LITTLE JOE
— THE —
WRANGLER

MIKE ALLISON

This book is dedicated to the memory of the men who rode their way into history, leaving behind the legend and the legacy that has become known the world over as the iconic symbol of a great nation, and to all those who strive each day to keep alive the Spirit of the Great American Cowboy.

PROLOGUE

I N THE THREE DECADES FOLLOWING the end of the Civil War, over ten million head of cattle were rounded up in Texas and other parts of the Southwest, and driven to markets and railheads in the north to feed a healing and hungry nation.

While many contributed to these enterprises, it is the role of the cowboy, whose courage and commitment is indelibly imprinted in our nation's memory.

Drawing from the skills honed by the Mexican vaquero, these brave men endured months on end of hot, dirty, and dangerous work as they drove herds numbering in the thousands north on the Goodnight-Loving, the Chisholm, and other lesser known trails.

They came from all walks of life, but they lived and died with one common trait: a can do, never quit attitude.

This is the story of one them.

This is the story of all of them.

CHAPTER ONE

JOE

DAWN WAS BREAKING OVER THE East Texas pines. The grey slowly ebbed to reveal a pitiful shotgun house that by all appearances had been pitiful for a good long while, though the state of its decrepitude appeared to have advanced considerably recently. It was a testament to the power of the wilderness in this part of the country — how quickly the inroads of civilization, even when not partial and incomplete, were beaten back. The house, not quite finished, had begun its decline already. The front door was sagging, no longer quite plumb, and no longer able to be shut completely. Two sides of the house had a thin coat of whitewash. One side, the northern side, had been only partially whitewashed, about a third of it unfinished, and that part had already taken the semblance of age, grey and weathered. The fourth side had nothing and was showing the same wear.

Off to the side of the house was a barn that was built around the same time as the house, but had somehow found a way to look in an even worse state of disrepair. A weathervane stood atop the barn, but it was bent, stooped like the fencing that surrounded the dilapidated corrals on either side of the barn.

The quiet of the morning was pierced by the crow of a solitary rooster, strutting alone, with no hens to show off for. He strutted and he clucked and he paused then crowed again, as if he expected a different outcome. Still no hens.

A windmill stood between the house and barn, working but just barely, with a couple of the blades missing and one that had somehow gotten bent. There was generally not much wind in the mornings, and this morning was no exception. So the windmill just stood there, yet another monument to neglect and inattention.

Behind the house, not too far from the small creek that ran roughly parallel to it, was an outhouse. It seemed the only structure on the place into which much diligence and craftsmanship went. There was pride in the intricate design of the crescent moon and three stars on the door. Whether or not it was a luxurious indulgence could be a matter of opinion, but there certainly was no doubt that this door was store bought.

A ray of sunlight gently found its way into the otherwise dark room where Joe Beauchamp, a rail-thin boy of about ten or eleven, slept a fitful and shallow sleep. The makeshift window shade was made out of a burlap feed sack imprinted with *Gunderson's Feed* in large red letters.

Gunderson's was but one of a number of enterprises which carried past due balances extended to Jack Beauchamp. Founded two dozen years ago by Lars Gunderson, patriarch of the Gunderson clan of Norwegians who had settled East of Dallas in Kaufman County, the venerable feed store served as a jumping off point for many of the farmers and small ranchers who came to settle in East Texas. Generous to a fault, Lars had somehow let Beauchamp smooth talk his way into far more credit than Jack's pitiful ranch could ever hope to repay. When Lars finally cut him off, his smug and satisfied demeanor left no doubt that Lars had been played false by a man whose word and bond was no good. Beauchamp promised to make good on the balance within the month, but when Lars went out to his place, axe handle in hand for extra persuasion, Jack was nowhere to be found.

The feed sack covering the window did a pretty lousy job keeping the mosquitoes out, but was very effective at keeping the heat in, even on a reasonably pleasant spring morning such as that one.

Sleeping restlessly, his face moistened with sweat, Joe instinctively swatted with his hand at a mosquito buzzing near his face. He rolled over in bed, which caused a deep sigh and pained grimace. The rope lattice which supported Joe on his homemade mattress, stuffed with moldy hay, creaked as he turned.

In the other room, just outside Joe's room, his stepmother furiously swept a clean floor. A nearly empty whiskey bottle sat on the small table beside the chair by the fireplace. An empty companion sat on the table in the kitchen.

Given her disheveled appearance, her dress tattered and dirty, her hair a mess, looking as though she had neither slept nor bathed in quite some time, one had to wonder about the source of this obsession with a clean floor. Perhaps it wasn't the floor at all but rather the distraction that the broom provided. She was agitated and distracted, but the cause of her irritation was not clear. The more she swept the angrier she became, and her sweeping became quicker and shorter and the strokes more angry. Quicker, angrier until it reached a fever pitch.

And she stopped, breathing heavily, silent and still for a moment.

Then just as suddenly as she had stopped sweeping, anger boiled over like a pot on a stove, and she strode uneasily the few steps to Joe's room, broom in hand, and threw open the door. In one short motion she reached his bed and hit him hard with the broom three times before he could get out of the way.

"Get up, you lazy snip!" she yelled, her words both snarled and slurred.

It was clear from how quickly Joe awoke, and how shallow his sleep had been, that this wasn't the first time he'd been visited upon by his stepmother and her broom.

"No! Please don't!" Joe pleaded as he scrambled to escape the broom.

"You don't work, you don't eat!"

Thankfully, she had to use the broom to steady herself, giving Joe a chance to quickly pull on his britches before she could take another swing.

"Your Pa might be a worthless good-for-nothin', but it'll be a cold day in Hell 'fore I let you be a loafer", she said.

Joe grabbed his hat and shoes, slipped by her as she took another swing with the broom, narrowly missing him. He ran from the room and out the door, heading in the direction of the barn.

His stepmother took a couple of quick steps in the direction Joe had headed, but thought better of it as a deep queasiness began to menace her stomach.

She staggered out onto the front porch, her face pale as

the moonlight of the night just ended. As Joe was running toward the barn, barefoot and still carrying his shoes, she yelled after him, "Get them cows milked first, and then get to cleanin' them chicken coops!"

Tears unseen by his stepmother streaming down his face, Joe ran into the barn.

Once inside, he stopped and looked around, fixing his gaze on the milking stool near the stalls where the two milk cows were kept. He took a seat on the stool as he began to catch his breath. He slowly put on his shoes. Brogans they were, both identical – neither right nor left – and both uncomfortable.

The two Holstein cows looked identical for the most part, unusual for the black and white breed, and only Joe could consistently tell them apart. They watched Joe put on his shoes, unimpressed by his presence. He'd named them Bitter and Sweet, names his stepmother had said were nonsensical,

He liked them. They were calm. He liked to milk them too, especially on cold winter mornings when he could be close enough to them to feel the comfort of the warmth of their bodies.

Joe got up and grabbed a pitchfork and proceeded to toss some hay into the girls' stalls. Then he walked to the rack where he kept the pails he used for milking. He always cleaned the pails and set them out the night before so he wouldn't have to take the time to bother with them in the morning.

He grabbed the pail, then picked up the stool he'd been sitting on and went over to Bitter. He placed the stool near her udders and the pail under them, sat down and started milking. He always started with Bitter before going on to milk Sweet. He didn't really know why. It was just the routine he'd seemed to settle into. Most days, Sweet gave a pail full, and Bitter somewhat less. Today was a good day for Bitter and she matched Sweet's output, making the two pails in tandem quite heavy for Joe's spindly arms to carry.

As he slowly trudged toward the house, shoulders stooped by the weight of the milk laden pails, he stubbed a toe on a small rock, causing him to spill some of the milk from both pails.

"Oh, no", he muttered.

He cast a quick, furtive glance at the house, silently praying she didn't see. He saw no sign of her and he allowed himself to exhale. He knew that she'd notice that some of the milk was missing when she went out on the porch to get the milk for use in her butter making, and he knew that would be the excuse she'd use to beat him. But as long as she didn't see, there was a chance he'd get a reprieve for the day. A small chance, but a chance nonetheless.

The morning wore on slowly as Joe tried to forget his growling stomach and the fact that he'd not been allowed to eat breakfast. Cleaning the chicken coops was the chore he hated the most. While the smell of cattle and horses seemed quite natural to Joe, chickens and the smell of their dung made him feel light-headed and weak in the knees. Not only that, they pecked his hands. Pecked when he went in to clean their coops. Pecked when he went in to gather eggs. He wasn't the type to wish ill on any of God's creatures, but he thought often how much he enjoyed the chicken his stepmother fried up on Sundays.

As he finished up the cleaning of the coops, the thoughts of Sunday fried chicken reminded him of how hungry he was. The thunder in his belly, a periodic, audible reminder of that hunger, seemed to get louder with each occurrence, those which were growing in frequency as the morning slowly passed.

Reluctantly, Joe walked over to the woodpile next to the house. He picked up the axe that was leaning up against the large stump that his Pa used for wood splitting. The axe was way too heavy for Joe to swing with accuracy, but he gamely went to work at splitting the logs in the pile. Thankfully, his Pa had spent a good bit of time sharpening the blade before he left. He spent a lot of time sharpening the blade of his axe, often staying in the barn late into the evening. Joe often wondered if he enjoyed the peace of the rhythmic motion of the blade on the large whetstone. Perhaps it gave him some respite from the constant harpings of Joe's stepmother.

Even though the larger logs were beyond Joe's capacity to split, he could manage, barely and with much frustration, some of the smaller ones. Lost in his thoughts, he reached to grab another log. There just inside the pile, a copperhead was disturbed by Joe's movement. He froze, and in his mind he heard the phrase every boy and girl he knew had been taught.

Red and yellow, kill a fellow.

Red and black, friend of Jack.

This was no milk snake, and Joe knew it. Before he could pull his hand away, the snake slivered away, quickly, back into the shade. Joe exhaled the breath he didn't realize he was holding, and heard his stepmother's voice from the house.

"Come eat!"

Joe walked quickly to the house, his hunger getting the better of the dread of his stepmother's mood. He wasn't really sure if it was the drinking that made her angry, or if she drank because she was angry. But he did know that anger and bitterness were her usual state of being lately, no matter what he did or how hard he tried to please her.

Joe walked in the door and quietly sat down at the table, eagerly awaiting the mid-day meal.

His stepmother said, "What took you so long?" as she glanced over her shoulder.

"I hurried as fast as I could," said Joe.

She put a plate of food in front of him. Cornbread, some bacon that bordered on rancid, a pool of gravy with the last bits of the squirrel she'd shot three days ago. Joe started eating ravenously, consuming quickly both from hunger and the uncertainty of how long he'd be allowed to stay at the table.

"Do you think Pa will be back today?" said Joe, with a mouthful of food.

"I've about give up on him ever comin' back."

She stared blankly through the door and out onto the porch. "Shouldn't have took him more'n a week to get to Greenville and back, and now it's been a month."

She stood still for another moment, remaining in a contemplative state, her gaze not leaving the door.

"He said he'd come back, but I could tell."

Her jaw clenched a little. "I could tell."

She clenched her jaw more tightly, then clenched her fists

as her mood changed from something akin to resignation to just plain mad and she grew increasingly agitated.

Joe kept eating, shoveling as rapidly as he could, as though he knew what was coming.

The woman angrily knocked the plate away and onto the floor.

"Back to work, you miserable wretch," she said, with a cruelty in her voice that was more pronounced than he we used to.

If anyone else had been around to see the combination of fear and sadness in Joe's eyes as he looked up at her, it would have moved them and touched their humanity. Joe's stepmother was not moved.

Night fell and brought the end of what had become a normal day. Joe hadn't had supper, though he didn't think his stepmother had eaten either. In fact, he couldn't remember the last time he'd seen her eat any food at all, though he allowed that he spent most of his daytime hours outdoors doing chores, not within eyesight of her. He was happy that he'd been able to scoop up a sizable piece of the cornbread and some of the bacon from the floor earlier as he dashed out of the house after his abbreviated mid-day meal. He ate it on the run so she wouldn't see. Having that helped, but he lay in bed, still hungry.

Outside on the porch, on a hanging swing, his stepmother was sprawled out, asleep and smelling of piss and vomit, a bottle of whiskey clutched in her hand with just a few swallows remaining in it. Her breathing was deep, punctuated by periodic snores that were so loud as to rival any man. Suddenly, she snorted and nearly woke herself. But she soon settled back down into her deep rhythmic breathing.

Joe carrying a small satchel, tiptoed out the door and past her, quietly making his way to the barn. Once inside, he lit a dim lantern, illuminating the inside of the barn. He went to corner where an old saddle sat on a rack, long unused and covered in dust. The leather on the saddle was extremely dried and cracked. Joe wondered if it would be so loud and creaky as to give him away as he pulled it down from the rack, when he began saddling up Chaw, his brown pony, as quietly as he could.

"Don't know where we're goin', Chaw, but any place has gotta be better than here."

He snuffed out the lantern and led the pony to the barn door which he slowly swung open. He slipped a canteen over the saddle horn and mounted up. Joe rode Chaw away from the barn, taking care to walk him as slowly as he could to keep the saddle leather and the pony's footfalls silent.

Joe's stepmother snorted again, this time waking herself up. She clumsily got up from the porch swing, bottle still in hand. She stumbled into the house and picks up a fireplace poker on her way to Joe's room.

She kicked the door open and stumbled to Joe's bed. She whacked the bed with the iron poker where Joe should have been sleeping, her face registering surprise when she realized the bed was empty.

"Now where'd you get off to?" she asked, her chest heaving from the exertion.

CHAPTER TWO

BEN

WHEN ONE SPENDS A WEEK on a train, there's a lot
to see. And young Ben, a tall, lanky boy of eighteen
had certainly seen a lot already. With just a few
hours or so to go until his arrival in Fort Worth, he was
sure things would continue to be interesting. He ran his
fingers through his dark brown hair and tugged at the high,
starched collar that chafed his neck.

Ben pulled his journal out of the valise that sat next to
his feet and began to peruse the notes he'd taken over the
course of his journey thus far. He felt someone staring at
him, and as he looked up, he caught the briefest of glimpses
of the beautiful raven-haired young lady across the aisle
and two rows down. She was looking at him, or was she?
Perhaps it was his imagination. He averted his eyes so as
not to appear eager or impolite.

He looked through the pages, recalling as he read the
many characters and bits of landscape he'd seen on his trip.
There was the fat, sloppy bald man who plopped down
next to him, his neck spilling out over his collar. For some
interminable period of time, the man, smelling of sweat

and vaguely of urine, seemed bound and determined to occupy every inch of his seat and half of Ben's. He was a companion not missed when he disembarked.

Ben felt it again. He looked up. His heart skipped. She was looking at him, though she quickly she turned her eyes away.

He went back to his journal, but was unable to concentrate very well. He recalled the elderly woman and her even more elderly husband. He had thought she bore a striking resemblance to a dried persimmon, and Ben couldn't understand how someone so petite and fragile could have the energy to be so persistent in the haranguing of her husband. She reminded him not to forget to check all the bags at the hotel and to make sure the bellman didn't steal anything, that he used the bathroom before the train started moving again, and, several times, to move his legs so they wouldn't be stiff when he got off the locomotive. It was quite clear that he was well practiced in the art of playing deaf. The more she went on, the more aggressively he ignored her. The more he ignored her, the louder she got. The louder she got, the quieter his eventual answer was. It occurred to Ben that it may have been some sort of game to the old gentleman, a way to pass the time on the journey, not just the train but on the very long journey of his life.

He felt it again and looked up. There they were, those beautiful greens eyes staring.

Only this time, she didn't look away. Nor did Ben. They held each other's gaze for what seemed to Ben, a heavenly eternity.

Then she smiled at him. A demure, polite smile. Ben

returned the smile, and regretting that he had no hat to tip, nodded to her.

A sharp elbow from the young lady's mother put an end to the exchange, but the effect lasted for the rest of the trip. He'd been around young ladies before and even fancied a couple, but this encounter made him feel... Well he wasn't sure how it made him feel, he just knew that he liked it, a lot.

It made him think how wonderful and full of surprises, both pleasant and otherwise, his new life could be. How many men he might get to know and what they might have to teach him? How many women he might meet, not just pretty young girls, but also women in the kinds of places he'd only heard about but not yet seen? Yes, a new and exciting adventure lay ahead.

Ben was jolted back to the current by the booming voice of the conductor shouting, "Arriving in Fort Worth!"

He grabbed his valise and started to make his way to the end of the car, hoping to grab one more glimpse at the beauty that had made the last part of the train ride so pleasant. Alas, she was nowhere to be found. The thought occurred to him that her mother had hurried away so as to not encourage any more interaction between the two. He looked at his suit, a bit wrinkled from the trip, but still sharp for the most part and thought to himself that he didn't present too disappointing a figure.

Ben stepped off the train in Fort Worth and inquired at the station for directions to the address where his uncle had indicated in his letter that a horse would be waiting for him.

As he walked along the thoroughfare, he was struck by how quiet the streets were. Compared to St. Louis, Fort

Worth seemed quite tranquil. Granted, it was Sunday morning. He saw the occasional buggy or buckboard trot past. There were a handful of couples strolling down the walkway. Two ladies carried parasols, which likely did little to defend against the heat of the strong morning sun. A few gentlemen has pistols holstered on their hips to repel some unknown threat. Otherwise, there wasn't much activity. In the distance, but not too far away by his judgment, the sound of a piano and clumsy voices singing along to it, disturbed the peace.

"Must be the place," Ben thought to himself.

The sign, painted a garish red and yellow, read "Fincher's Horse and Tack Emporium". Below the sign, a storefront served as entranceway to the stables behind. A tall, lanky, reed of a man sat in front of the store, expressing his frustration with the leather punch he was using to work on the headstall in his hand. He was using language even more colorful than the sign, which seemed out of place on a Sunday morning.

"Mornin' sir," Ben said.

The man looked up but didn't speak. He did grin in a way that bothered Ben a bit, though he wasn't sure why it did. His chin was tobacco-stained and the teeth that were still there were well past yellow, on their way to a brownish hue.

"Would you by any chance be able to direct me to Mr. Fincher?" Ben felt more nervous than he thought he should.

"That'd be me." Fincher said as he stood up.

Ben extended his hand. "My name is…"

"You Emmett's nephew?"

After a moment's hesitation, Ben said, "Yes sir. I am."

Fischer took his hand, strongly but with some indifference.

"How'd you know?"

"Your uncle wrote me," Fincher said, as he sized up Ben.

"Said you'd be a might on the green side."

Ben squirmed a little.

"Said he reckoned you'd be duded up too."

Ben hadn't been conscious of his clothes up to that point. It didn't occur to him how inappropriate they might be for the job ahead.

"My uncle told me that you'd…"

"Yep." said Fincher.

Ben thought to himself that the fellow sure wasn't shy about interrupting folks.

"Come on back. Got a horse for ya. Emmett already paid for him."

Ben followed Fincher back to the stables. "Been doin' business with your uncle for a lot 'o years. Usually gets the better of me." He grinned that grin again. "But not always."

He pointed out a bay gelding with a narrow strip of white running down the front of his head and white socks on both hind legs.

"Yonder he his. Rode him this morning and he's good and sound."

Fincher pointed at a saddle on a rack off to the side.

"That's yours with the horse, the bridle too." He said as he picked up a makeshift rope halter and walked toward the corral where the horse was eyeing him warily. He caught the horse and quickly slipped the halter on his head, then turned to lead him out. The horse balked a little, nervous at the thought of leaving.

"You sure he's well broken?" Ben said as he pulled the saddle off the rack.

"Aww, sure his is. To hear your uncle tell it, you'll be headin' up the Chisolm with the Bar Nothin' along with the rest of the trail hands. What are you frettin' about?"

There was that grin again. Ben wondered what he'd gotten himself into.

"He needs shoes, so you'll need to take him down to the farriers at the south end of the thoroughfare."

Ben began to saddle the horse.

"If I was you, I'd cinch him good and loose, and just lead him there. He ain't much for bein' barefoot." Almost to himself he said, "Learned that the hard way."

Ben was starting to think that Fincher was funning with him.

"Oh, I'll be alright. If I'm gonna ride him to Lampasas, I might was well get to know him." Ben said, feigning matter of factness, though the butterflies were already stampeding in his stomach.

Though not as practiced as he might like to be, Ben made sure he was particular about how he saddled the horse and just as particular how he put on the bridle. He didn't want to betray his lack of experience beyond what Fincher already thought he knew.

"My uncle said that a couple of the boys…"

"Yep. They're sleepin' off a good time at the Dove last night and will meet you here around mid-day to show you down to the Bar Nothin'. If they don't show I'll send for 'em. Before you get back, I'll fetch you some duds for the trail, like your uncle asked me to."

Having finished saddling his new horse, Ben led him

out front with Fincher following. Ben prepared to put his left foot in the stirrup and mount up but the horse shied away a little. Fincher grinned that grin.

"Whoa." Ben said as he tried to calm the horse and make another attempt. This time he got his foot in the stirrup and quickly swung his right leg over. The horse reared up as Ben fished for his other stirrup with his right foot, catching it just in time to pull both feet behind him and keep from falling over the cantle of his saddle.

The effort seemed enough to settle the horse and he stood on his four feet, a little skittish, but manageable for Ben.

"Is there a church around here I might go to?" said Ben.

"A couple of 'em. You'll pass one on your way." Fincher said, calling after him as he headed off in the direction of the farrier.

Once he'd dropped the horse off at the farrier, having negotiated the thoroughfare with some effort, Ben found he had a couple of hours to kill. He had suspected he would. Looking back up the thoroughfare, he saw quite a large number of people filing into the church he'd passed on his way from Fincher's. It looked quite inviting, and, not knowing when he'd get another chance to sit in a proper church and listen to a proper sermon, he decided to join in.

As he sat through the sermon, he tried to block out the distractions in his mind, the journey on the train, Fincher, his new mount, the ride down to the Bar Nothin', the drive back up north with the herd, his uncle whom he hadn't seen since he was ten or thereabouts.

The pastor seemed quite vigorous in the delivery of his message. Ben took some comfort in at least being able to notice, and hopefully recall, that aspect of the sermon. The words however, seemed a jumble of baritone punctuated by the occasional clap of thunder. Something about decadence, and Hell's Half Acre, and turning away from the temptations of a sinful city.

After a while, the sermon came to a rousing conclusion, complete with vigorous head nodding and numerous utterances of "Amen!" from the congregation.

At least he went, thought Ben. And at least he could truthfully write to his mother and tell her he went.

The congregation stood and started toward the door. Ben filed out with them. Just outside, the pastor stood to meet and greet. The man stopped Ben with a hand extended, in offer of a handshake.

"Thank you for a great sermon, Pastor."

"Well thank you, young man." He sized Ben up and said, "you're a new face."

"Yes, sir. My name is Ben. I'm just passing through on my way to my new situation."

Other churchgoers file out, some seemingly annoyed by the pastor's attention on Ben. Some head over to the community area next to the church building. It was a nice area with some large shade trees and a number of tables, quite a few with picnic baskets on them.

"You seem a man of letters. Are you educated?"

"I'm not sure, sir. I've had some schooling," Ben said.

"Would you be on your way to teach school?"

"No sir. Nothing that fancy. I'm going to work for the Bar Nothin' Ranch, down near Lampasas."

"I see. Will you…"

Vernon Tidwell and his family had made their way through the door of the church, to the pastor and Ben. A large and loud man, Vernon moved as if he was unaccustomed to having anyone stand in his way, as though his mere presence should serve to part the waters, or the people. Mrs. Tidwell, matronly and robust, was close on his heels. Though a bit more mannerly in her comportment, it was clear from her demeanor that she was cut from the same cloth as her husband. Their daughter Lucy followed behind, along with her two younger brothers. A petite and very fetching girl of sixteen, Lucy had auburn hair tied with ribbons and crystal blue eyes that had an arresting effect on anyone who gazed in them.

Tidwell and his wife brusquely shouldered Ben aside, interrupting his conversation with the pastor.

"Excellent sermon as always, Reverend. Just excellent," said Tidwell with his characteristic bellowing tone.

"I made you a pecan pie. I know it's your favorite," said Mrs. Tidwell.

"Oh that's wonderful. Thank you!" said the pastor, thinking he did not want to appear as rude as the Tidwells.

Lucy, looking past her parents and the pastor, demurely smiled at Ben as he receded from the group, backing out the door of the vestibule and into the courtyard of the church. Ben shyly smiled back, but clearly felt out of place. Mrs. Tidwell took note of the exchange.

The pastor also noticed Ben leaving and called to him over the din of the congregants.

"Ben, please do stay for the picnic. You're a welcome guest."

"Thank you, sir," Ben said, not knowing what else to say.

Ben awkwardly made his way over to the picnic area. He nodded to a couple of the churchgoers, as he wandered around looking for a place to sit.

Ben felt a hand on his shoulder. Startled, he turns to see that it was the pastor, followed closely by Mrs. Tidwell and two companions.

"Ben, let me introduce you to some of my congregation. This is Mrs. Stilton. And Mrs. Johnson. And this is Mrs. Tidwell."

He turned to the women. "Ladies, this is our young visitor, Ben."

Ben and the ladies exchange "How do you do's?"

"Ben is a man of letters," said the pastor.

"Well, I wouldn't say…" started Ben, trying to correct him. But it was too late. The pastor walked away to speak with some other members of his congregation.

"Oh that's marvelous, Ben," said Mrs. Tidwell.

"How many years have you studied?" asked Mrs. Stilton.

"Are you a teacher?" asked Mrs. Johnson.

The ladies continued peppering Ben with questions, not apparently caring what the answers would be, certainly not enough to give him the time to properly answer before getting interrupted by the next question.

As the ladies continued to interrogate Ben, Lucy was talking with her friend, Rachel Stilton, and watching the interview from some distance away across the community park.

"Looks like the hens have found a new worm to peck at," said Lucy.

"I'm not sure which one is worse, your mother or mine," Rachel said with a subtle giggle. "Neither can hold a candle to old Mrs. Johnson though."

"Oh, that's for certain," Lucy said. She looked across the way at Ben who was visibly uncomfortable with all the attention he was receiving from the trio of matrons.

"Please do sit down and have some chicken," said Mr. Stilton.

"No thank you ma'am. I really must be going. I still have quite some distance to travel to my new employer." Ben paused, not sure if this is the opening to make his leave that he was hoping for.

"It was very nice to make your acquaintance, ladies," he said.

He regretted yet again that he had no hat to tip to the women. He had the good sense not to wait for a response and started walking toward the gate leading out to the thoroughfare.

Ben sighed in relief as he approached the gate, strangely emboldened by how he handled the awkward encounter with the older ladies. He noticed Lucy and her friend whispering and looking at him. He paused, gathered his courage, and then walked toward them.

"Afternoon, girls." Ben nodded to the young ladies. "Fine day is it not?" he added.

The girls giggled nervously.

"My name is Ben. And you are?"

"I am…" began Rachel.

Lucy nudges her friend with a not so gentle elbow.

"…going. I see my mother could use some help setting up the lunch," interrupted Lucy.

Rachel scurried away, briefly looking over her shoulder once, and left Lucy alone with Ben.

"I'm Lucy. Pardon my friend. She's a bit shy."

Ben nodded his acknowledgement.

"It is a fine day. Will you be joining us for our after church picnic?"

"Well I'd surely like to. The pastor invited me, but I really ought to be on my way. I stopped in for the service but have a long ride ahead of me, if I'm to get to my new situation on schedule," said Ben.

"Oh. Where is your new employer, if I may be curious?"

"The Bar Nothin' Ranch, near Lampasas. I'll only just report in and then the drive will head north for Abilene," he said. "Kansas." He first thought he ought to clarify the state, but immediately regretted it for the awkwardness it created.

"A cattle drive? What will you be doing on a cattle drive? You don't look like a cowboy."

"What is a cowboy supposed to look like?" said Ben, a bit sheepishly.

"My uncle Emmett is the Trail Boss and he's taking me with him. It's my first trip. Hopefully not my last."

"It is dangerous work, as I understand."

"I suppose so," he said. "I spent the last week on a train from St. Louis."

"St. Louis! That sounds exciting," she said. "Is that where you are from?"

"Yes it is. I live there with my mother. She and my father owned an apothecary. Well, she still does." Ben grew frustrated with how confused he must have sounded to the girl he so wanted to like him.

"My father passed."

"Oh, I'm sorry to hear it," she said.

An uncomfortable pause crept up and intruded into

the conversation. After what seemed to Ben an eternity, he decided he had to take a chance. He would regret if he didn't.

"I apologize for being so bold, but time isn't on my side, and I think you're prettier than a flower in the morning dew." The boldness of his statement, and the fact that he had actually said it out loud, caught him more by surprise than it did Lucy. Although they both blushed, his was the more crimson.

"I have to go pick up my horse from the farrier but before I go, I must ask…" His heart was racing and he felt sort of dizzy. "…do you have a beau?" he asked.

Lucy was already blushing, but the question prolonged it.

"Well, no I don't. But my father would have something to say about that at any rate."

Ben paused awkwardly, struggling to speak.

"Would it be acceptable to you if I were to ask your father for permission to court you?" he asked.

Lucy was clearly smitten, and she had much difficulty maintaining an appropriate level of propriety in her response. She was quite fearful that her response would be unduly forward.

"Nothing would please me more, young Mr. Ben."

Ben smiled with satisfaction. It was not the smile one would show as a result of a successful conquest, but rather a smile of genuine happiness. He really was impressed by Lucy. He wanted to get to know her better and he was quite glad of the prospect of doing so.

"I will return from the farrier within the hour and do just that then, Miss Lucy."

Lucy returned the smile. Hers was just as genuine.

"I will make you a passel of food for your journey."

Ben fetched his freshly shod mount from the farrier and swapped his valise and traveling suit for a bedroll, canteen, and some duds more appropriate for the trail. These included a decent, though not so gently used, pair of boots, some dungarees, and thankfully, a hat. Fincher told him that the previous owner had been a bit unlucky, dying without the boots on his feet, and another of the smiles followed. Ben wasn't sure he believed him, given that grin. However, the fact that Fincher glanced over at the Dove when he said it, and the Dove being one of the more notorious houses of ill repute in town, there was some credence to the statement. Ben wasn't particularly keen on wearing a dead man's boots but he didn't have time to argue the point. He planned to return to the church picnic to speak to Lucy's father as he'd promised he would. He was quite pleased that his prospective traveling companions had yet to show, giving him time to do so.

As Ben approached the church, he was grateful that his horse had settled into his handling which made for a more pleasant and, insofar as his reputation amongst strangers as a horseman was concerned, far less risky ride up the thoroughfare. He dismounted and tied his horse to the hitching post, then walked toward the picnic which seemed to be winding down. Ladies were packing up baskets and gentlemen were smoking cigars.

As he approached the gate, Ben saw Mrs. Tidwell whispering to Mr. Tidwell, who appeared agitated. He walked confidently up to the gate of the courtyard where he was met by Mr. Tidwell.

"Would you be Lucy's father, sir?" Ben extended his hand. Mr. Tidwell did not take it.

"Save your breath and save your steps, son," Tidwell said, his voice dripping with disdain. "You can turn around and get right back on that horse."

"I don't understand, sir. I'm not sure what impression you have, but I assure you that my intentions with your daughter are entirely honorable."

"Your intentions are not my concern, young man. However, your pretenses at present, are."

Ben hesitated, the sudden turn of events having left him largely speechless for the moment.

"Sir, I…"

Lucy rushed up to the men, followed closely by her mother.

"Father, no! Ben is quite a nice young man and he's been nothing but a perfect gentleman." She cast her glance first at Ben, who was perplexed. Then she looked at her father. "He was coming to ask your permission to court," Lucy said with a slight tone of rebellion.

"Oh, I'm quite aware of his intentions," said Tidwell. "Mark my words, young lady; no daughter of mine will ever be courted by one such as him. He sat through the pastor's sermon today, and then right afterward commenced to present himself as a lettered man."

"Sir, I never…" said Ben, trying to defend himself. Tidwell would hear none of it.

"Rather then, he's just a saddle tramp, a ruffian,"

he said. Tidwell jerked his head in the direction of Ben, directing Lucy to look. "I mean, look at him."

Ben now regretted changing out of his traveling suit and into his trail clothes. *This has gone very, very wrong*, Ben thought to himself.

"Father, he is so much more. Won't you give him a chance?" Lucy said.

"A chance? There is no chance that he will ever be worthy of you. He will never hold a station that would allow him to adequately provide for you," said Tidwell. He turned toward Ben.

"You may have a silver tongue, young man, but it *is* forked, and I demand that you refrain from further contact with my daughter." He glared at Ben in a way that meant business. It was clear to Ben that this was a man who was used to running over people, a man who always got his way.

"Now please leave," said Tidwell, his voice raised enough to catch the attention of some of the other picnic – goers.

Ben, knowing what he was up against, yet knowing also that he was in the right, gathered his wits despite Tidwell's onslaught.

"Sir, the good pastor invited me here, and I am here by his graciousness and generosity."

"Young man, I am telling you in the most serious of terms that you will stay away from my daughter."

"Sir, I may not be worthy of your daughter, but I *will* be a success someday. When I am, I will return for her, and she can decide my worthiness. With or without your acceptance, we will court, and perhaps some day marry."

"You will do no such thing," said Tidwell, seething.

Ben turned to look at Lucy.

"I very much doubt that I would be allowed to correspond directly with you here. But I will do my best to check the post in Fort Worth when the drive passes near. If you meant what you said earlier, I would be most honored to have a letter from you there. Ben Montrose, care of Emmett Logan of the Bar Nothin' Ranch."

Mr. Tidwell's anger was boiling over and his fists were clenched. Ben looked blankly at him, unfazed or so it appeared to Tidwell, and then smiled at Lucy and tipped his hat to her.

"Good day, Miss Lucy. I will see you again if you will have me do so."

Lucy returned the smile and her father turned his angry glare in her direction.

CHAPTER THREE

JAVIER

I T WAS A SULTRY EVENING for the springtime, even in South Texas where Javier Rodriguez and his wife Rosa had made their home, just a few hundred acres, but adjacent to open range and close enough to decent water to make the place worthwhile. A number of high fenced corrals surrounded the modest three room house that Javier and two of his cousins had built.

Javier was a solid young man of Mexican descent, not thin, but not heavy set either. At twenty-eight he was beginning to show the wear of the sun and years on the cattle trail. Rosa was several years younger than Javier and they'd married when she was seventeen in a grand wedding in San Antonio, befitting Rosa's prominent family. Javier did not come from money, but he was descended from a family of proud Tejanos, Texans of Mexican descent, many of whom fought against Santa Anna's Mexico in the war of Texas independence. They had been proud citizens of the Republic of Texas. His family pooled their resources to help get the young couple off to a decent, if meager start. It wasn't much but enough to buy some land and the materials Javier used to build the house, the barn and corrals.

Rosa was the last of her father's four daughters to get married, and he was in no hurry to see her off to the life of a married woman. However, he did think highly of Javier and wanted to see him do well for himself. Roberto Gonzales was also the sort of man who believed that every man should be self-made, just as he was and his father was before him. All wealth should be bequeathed to the Church. Those were his family's firmly held beliefs. So there was no offering of assistance to Javier and Rosa in getting their start, and only a modest dowry for the marriage, despite her father's considerable wealth.

Proud as he was, Javier did have a slight tinge of bitterness on occasion when he thought of the resources lavished on such an extravagant wedding. All that for a single day, but nothing to help them once married. Still, it was Señor Gonzales' money and the man could spend it as he saw fit. For that Javier held no grudge. In fact, when he was out on the trail, or scouting alone for days at a time, he'd remember Rosa and how beautiful she was on that day. He'd think of how she grew more beautiful each day, as their love had deepened and matured.

As the sun was setting, Javier was bringing in the last of the horses. This last band consisted of about thirty head, which were mostly new to the herd and not yet accustomed to the daily routine. Gathering all the other horses first made gathering the last group a little easier, Horses being herd animals, they were naturally inclined to join the larger group, which was well over two hundred head. While a vaquero and scout of some renown amongst the bigger ranches in south and central Texas for quite some time, Javier had only more recently developed quite a reputation as an excellent horseman, and had begun to build a breeding program that held great promise. It was this, and his strong desire to do well for his beloved Rosa that drove his willingness to make the long and dangerous drives north for the big ranchers. He knew it would not have to be forever. While he was gone on the drives during the late spring and summer, he let most of the horses run free on the adjacent range land, as they would have to range wide to find enough grazing, particularly by the end of summer when grass was very hard to come by. Where they'd once been troublesome in terms of stealing horses, there weren't enough Comanches left to bother worrying about. Those who did remain knew and respected his brand.

He kept only the mares with new foals in close, so Rosa could see to them, and make sure they were able to run with the herd when they were ready. These were no mustangs and had been bred to be more docile and ready for the saddle, when they reached the age to be broken.

Given that it was his last night at home for quite some time, it took longer than Javier had wanted to get the last of the horses put up, but he eventually finished and then bedded down his saddle horse in the small barn near the house. He was bone tired from a long day, but stopped to draw a bucket of fresh water from the well to save Rosa the trouble. He drew a long and much needed drink from the ladle by the pump, then carried the bucket into the house. He knew supper would be waiting. He couldn't wait to eat, and to see his Rosa.

The house was dimly lit from the inside by just a couple

of coal oil lamps. The hour had grown late and the horses in the corrals were already quiet. Some of them were laying down, others sleeping where they stood.

In the main room of the house, lit by one of the lamps, Javier and Rosa were seated at the table having a quiet, but very intense discussion while Javier ate his supper.

"I don't want you to go. Why do you have to go?" Rosa asked.

"It's the last trip. After this I won't have to go again," Javier said.

"But you don't have to go this time. We can make out fine. You know we can."

"Rosa, we've talked about this. One more drive and we'll have enough horses to finish our herd."

"But the drive north is so dangerous. Then you have to turn around and drive the horses back with almost no help. It's so unwise. What if? What if you don't come back?"

"It's hard I know, but I can buy them so much cheaper at the end of the drive. Getting them home isn't easy, but it's the only way we can afford to do it."

"Please, Javi. Please don't go."

"One last trip," he said. "And we can work on a family. We can't give up. We just can't."

"Of course not," she said with a combination of resignation and resentment.

In the small lantern lit side room, Ellie, a thin girl, recently widowed and no older than seventeen, was slowly pacing back and forth holding Jeremiah. The armful was her towheaded, six month old baby boy, to whom she was quietly humming a lullaby. After a good long while after he'd fallen asleep, Ellie gently eased the baby down into the drawer of the chest, padded with blankets, which served as his makeshift crib. She placed a light blanket around him. Ellie silently left the room, joining Javier and Rosa in the main room.

"Finally got him to sleep," Ellie said.

"He was very cranky tonight," Rosa said.

"Worse than usual. I think he's still adjusting to my milk. Your cooking has taken some getting use to." She paused and then thought she should clarify. "Not that it isn't wonderful, Rosa, just a might spicy."

"I'd say you're settling in very well," Javier said.

"I am so grateful for you taking me in. Little Jeremiah and I had nowhere else to go," Ellie said to both of them, bowing her head with sadness and sighing heavily.

"Give it time, Ellie. It's not even been a year. Grieving is not easy," Javier said.

"I know. It's just that Adam died and never knew that he would have a child," she said. "Javier, I wish you wouldn't go. Rosa needs you here."

"I know she does. But I have to go. One more time I have to go. Besides, you'll look after her, won't you?"

"You know I will, and she after me."

"Of course I will," Rosa said, patting Ellie gently on the arm. "We'll take care of each other, and Jeremiah. And when Javi returns in the fall we will have a new start."

She turns to Javier. "You will keep your word to me, no? This is your last trip north?"

"That is my word, Rosalita."

Ellie rises to leave the room.

"I'm going to bed. The baby will wake to feed in a couple of hours."

"Get some rest. Buenos noches," Rosa said.

"Good night," Ellie said to Rosa.

"Buenos noches, Ellie," Javier said. "I will leave for Lampasas before first light in the morning, so farewell until I return in the fall."

"Be safe and come home to Rosa, as you said you would." Ellie's eyes glazed over and she quickly left the room before her tears spilled over.

"Poor child," said Rosa.

"Which one, Ellie or the baby?" asked Javier.

"Both, I suppose," Rosa said with a heavy sigh.

Crickets sang their familiar song as the moonlight shown on Javier's house. The moon was half full, and bright in the sky, except for some light clouds that passed slowly across it. Down on the dry ground, the air was very still. The lanterns went out inside the house and it was dark, except for the moonlight.

Rosa led Javier to the bed, gently holding his hand until they reached the foot of it. Then she turned to face him and put his hand to her breast. She removed her dress. He kissed her, sweetly at first. Then as his passion swelled, his kisses and those she returned, grew more urgent. Their love and passion took them to their bed and the moonlight encased them in its glow.

After a time that lasted longer and was more passionate than usual for them, the encounter ended with a beautiful finality that befit their last chance to touch for many months. Javier and Rosa separated and lay next to each other, both looking up at the ceiling, slowly recovering from the exertion.

"I am going to miss you so much," Javier said.

"Miss me or miss that?" Rosa said, somewhat matter-of-factly.

"Aren't they related?" Javier said, hoping that she didn't take his words as being as cold as they sounded to him.

Rosa sighed and rolled over to lay on his shoulder. She placed her hand on his chest, feeling it slowly rise and fall, missing him already.

"If I can't give you a son, then there isn't really anything else I can give you except that."

"Shh… Don't talk like that. We must keep believing that God will bless us."

"For years we have tried, and for years we have failed," she said.

"Yes," he said.

"Someday we must accept that for us, a family is not in God's plan."

"I can not accept that. I must have a son," he said, as he continued to stare at the ceiling. "I will continue to pray, and we will continue to try, and someday we will be blessed."

Tears welled up in Rosa's eyes, but Javier couldn't see them in the darkness. She sniffed from the runny nose that the tears have given her.

"I'm sorry, Javi."

Javier realized she was crying.

"Oh Rosa. I'll be gone for four or five months, maybe more. Please don't let your tears be the memory I take with me."

"I know. It's just I… I wish…" she said. Then she whispers, "Please don't go."

"Shh… Come now. Smile for me. Let me take your smile on the trail with me."

Rosa smiles weakly up at him.

"There now. That's my love," he said.

"Te adoro," she said.

"Te adoro demasiado," he replied back.

Javier smiled at Rosa and stroked her hair for a long time. For a few more precious hours, he would hold his precious Rosa. They fell asleep in each other's arms.

She was still sleeping when he rose to leave. It was like this every time he left. She was always slightly upset when she woke and he was gone, but the feeling would pass quickly as she was reminded that his last words to her were that he loved her and his last touch was to hold her in his arms.

As he rode away from the house, he glanced back and recalled those same thoughts as he fought back the feeling of sadness that threatened to overcome him. He pointed his horse in the direction of Lampasas.

CHAPTER FOUR

CAMP

PREPARATION FOR A CATTLE DRIVE was, in general, something akin to barely organized chaos. The upcoming drive from the Bar Nothin' was no exception. The drive promised to be a very large one, even by John Callaway's standards. His Bar Nothin', at over a thousand sections, a section equaling one square mile or 640 acres, was one of the larger ranches in Texas.

It was late in the afternoon and the dozen or so cowboys that would drive the herd north to the stockyards in Abilene, Kansas had been hard at it since first light. They were working from a makeshift camp far enough away from the big ranch house to appease Mrs. Callaway, a petite woman from Boston who didn't particularly care for the sight, sound, and smell of cattle, horses, or cowboys.

The boys were primarily concerned with two main activities, readying the remuda for the trail, and branding the last of the cattle with the distinctive Bar Nothin' brand, which looked more or less like the Greek letter theta.

Eight of the boys were branding the large longhorn cattle, mostly steers but some cows as well. They worked in two teams of four men, the beeves being so large as to require that many to rope, tie and brand. Averaging 1,500 to 2,000 pounds, with horns that ranged from six to eight feet tip to tip, the steers were quite a handful. The boys were thankful that most of them had been branded in prior years when they were younger and smaller. There were enough of them that were still to be branded, as well as a quite a few cows which were smaller, that the work was taking its toll on the boys.

Emmett Logan, the longtime trail boss for Mr. Callaway and the Bar Nothin' was overseeing the preparatory activities, as he did every year for the past decade. He was a small man in his late forties with a booming voice and a habit of keeping very detailed notes of all aspects of the many cattle drives he'd bossed for the Bar Nothin' over the years. This habit kept him in good stead with Mr. Callaway but sometimes got him a bit crossways with the cowhands who, on occasion, would remember certain events a bit differently. Still, the boys knew Emmett's journal was gospel.

He rode up to the branding teams on his second favorite horse that he called Knickers, a stout bay with a bright white blaze on his forehead and three high white stockings. As was his custom (some would call it superstition) he was saving his beloved Peanut, a peanut colored chestnut, for the first day of the drive. He felt it brought him, and the Bar Nothin', good luck. Cowboys are, by and large, a superstitious lot, and Emmett was no exception. If one were to ask him, though, he'd deny the fact.

He knew that given how late in the day it was, the branding boys were probably pretty well spent. He also knew that he needed them to finish soon. Emmett called out to Jip, one of the Callaway hands who would not be going on the drive. He would be staying home to tend to the livestock that would remain at the ranch. Jip was one of the three hands working on the ground, and there was another of the team working horseback.

"Jip, how many left 'til you're done?" he said.

"About a couple dozen or so, I think," Jip replied, grateful for the chance to step away from the steer that was giving them a good deal of trouble.

"Think you can finish before it's too dark to work? Moonlight won't do." Emmett said.

"It'll be tight but I think we can," Jip said, knowing that a reply in the negative would not have been well received. Emmett knew Jip was over-promising.

"Do the best you can. I don't particularly want to be branding cattle tomorrow. I want to get our count by dusk, bed 'em down, and be headed north by first light the day after," Emmett said. He turned his horse and headed in the direction of the makeshift round pen, where Mick Spivey, Deacon, and a couple of the other boys were working with the saddle horses.

"Yassir," Jip said, even though it wasn't likely that Emmett was still within earshot.

As Emmett approached the round pen and the remuda penned next to it, he called to Deacon above the din of lowing cattle, the noises of horses and men.

"Deacon!" he called.

"Yes, sir?" Deacon replied, stepping down, mid-mount, from the horse.

Spivey was the drive's wrangler in charge of the near hundred saddle horses that would serve as mounts for the fifteen cowboys on that drive. Each cowboy would have six or seven they would use, sometimes three or more in a day.

But it was Deacon that Emmett trusted the most when it came to horsemanship. Deacon was a black cowboy, taller than most, with skin weathered as would be expected of a man who had lived many years in the sun and the saddle. He had served with the 10th Cavalry of Fort Riley, Kansas for several years with great distinction before joining Emmett and Mr. Callaway on the Bar Nothin'. His reputation as a horseman wasn't the only thing Deacon was known for. His time with the 10th Cavalry had, along with most of the men in the outfit, given him a chance to prove his worth as a man, regardless of the color of his skin. Those men, called "buffalo soldiers", first by the native tribes of the Plains against whom they fought and then by others, came to be known for their bravery, courage, physical and mental strength, as well as their sense of duty to each other. Deacon was perhaps best known of the soldiers of the 10th Cavalry, most especially for his rectitude and sense of fairness and justice, those qualities being the source of his nickname. No one seemed to know his real name or where he'd come from before he joined the Army. Those who knew him, or knew of him, never felt the need to ask. Deacon was a man's man, held in high esteem by virtually everyone who took the time to get to know him.

"Gonna need at least eight real solid mounts for a new cowboy. Better'n green broke and get as much of the sass as you can out of 'em," Emmett said.

"New cowboy?" Deacon said. A hint of perturbation was in his voice, but his good natured demeanor and long time relationship with Emmett softened the tone.

"Long story. Just gentle up a few for me," Emmett said.

"Consider it done, Emmett," he replied. "Delbert comin' with us?"

"Wouldn't go north without him."

"That's just fine. Mighty fine," Deacon said. He nodded with great satisfaction at the confirmation, and he was looking forward to seeing his good friend whom he hasn't seen since the end of last year's drive.

The sun was setting as Delbert Montgomery, a sandy haired cowboy in his mid-thirties, tall and lean, approached the camp. Emmett was sitting by a small campfire, writing in his logbook and sipping from a coffee cup. Delbert reached the camp and dismounted. He tied off his horse loosely to a Mesquite tree branch a little bit removed from the campfire.

"Evenin', Emmett."

"Same to you, Delbert." He eyed the big bay horse Delbert was riding. "I see you're still riding Pete."

"Yeah. Well you know me... I've always been partial to straight bays," Delbert said.

Emmett grinned. "Plain to look and bigger hearted than most."

"It'll be my second drive with him. I surely hope he stays with me for a good long while," Delbert said.

"He's a fine lookin' horse, of that there's no doubt," Emmett said.

Delbert sat down next to Emmett by the campfire. He grabbed a cup that was near the coffee pot.

"Been as solid as they come. Wish we had a whole remuda just like him," Delbert said.

Emmett poured a drink of whiskey from a jug that had been at his feet into his cup and offered to pour from the jug into Delbert's cup.

"Thought we might have a little whiskey this evening 'fore we head north. Be quite a spell before we can imbibe again," Emmett said.

Delbert nodded his approval and put down the coffee pot he'd been just about to pour from. Emmett poured a generous bit of whiskey into his cup. Delbert took a drink from the cup, and as the whiskey burned first his throat and then down into his chest, he thought, *I've had worse rot gut, but it's been a long while.* "Emmett's a good man, but not much of one for spending money on decent whiskey."

"True and certain. You know that a sober drive is the only sort I've ever been on, or ever been willing to go on to tell the truth of it," Delbert said. "Speaking of... You hire Hucks McPherson on as Cosinero?"

"I did. I know he can be a might prickly," Emmett said. "I'll keep an eye on him and make sure he tends to his chuck and keeps his jug out of sight of the boys."

"He's a good feller, and a fine cook. Reliable too, for a man that's been known to pull pretty regular from a whiskey bottle," Delbert said. He put a small log on the fire and tended to it, livening the fire up a bit.

"I hired Mick Spivey on as wrangler," Emmett said.

Delbert looked a bit dejected, though he tried not to let his disappointment at the demotion show on his face. He'd been Emmett's wrangler and run the remuda for the last four years. He was still loyal but despite being as trail hardened as any cowboy, it did hurt. Delbert thought he'd done a good job for Emmett with the horses and didn't see why he was being slighted.

Delbert was fortunate to ride with Emmett, who had a unique view of the wrangler position and, therefore, was among the most successful of the trail bosses to take cattle north. Most trail bosses assigned the role of wrangler to a young, inexperienced cowboy, one who wasn't ready for the role of full-fledged drover. Emmett, on the other hand, had always put the remuda in the hands of an experienced hand, a man with more horse sense than the rest of the men on the drive and who could keep the horses sound enough to allow the men to work more cattle than on a typical drive. As a consequence, Emmett's drives were larger and more profitable for their sponsors than other trail bosses, making him a highly sought after leader.

Delbert took a long sip of whiskey from his cup, then another, this time finishing it, and stared at the fire. His chest didn't seem to burn as much this time.

"Delbert, you've been a darn good wrangler for me and you're about as good a horseman as I've known, 'cepting maybe Deacon or Javier, but I need you as my El Segundo now," Emmett said.

Delbert's face brightened, but again he tried to hide how he felt about it. "That was quite a turn," he thought. To go from thinking he was going back to just punching cows with the rest of the boys, to becoming second in command of the drive. He was indeed enough to make his head spin. The warmth of the whiskey didn't help matters either.

"I'm honored, Emmett."

"It's well deserved, no doubt. We've got a hell of a drive ahead of us. It's the biggest herd I've ever taken north for the Bar Nothin'. Mr. Callaway said it might be one of the biggest anybody's ever driven. Over forty-five hundred head, maybe five thousand. Plus whatever range cows we pick up along the way," Emmett said.

Emmett finished the whiskey in his cup and pours himself some more. He held the jug out to Delbert, who moved his cup close enough for Emmett to pour a generous serving.

"Why so many on this drive?" Delbert asked.

"Mr. Callaway seems to think that this trip will be pretty rough. Probably lose quite a few on the way. More than usual," Emmett said. "But he says if that's true, then prices should still be pretty high by the time we get to Abilene."

"Why's that?" Delbert asked.

"Supply and demand, he says. He figures if it's so dry that we have a hard time, it'll likely stay that way all spring and everybody else will have trouble too," Emmett said.

"That's why he's the rancher and we're the hired hands," Delbert said.

Delbert and Emmett both sipped their whiskey, silently acknowledging the truth of Delbert's statement, and all the danger and hardship that would come with it.

"Ain't gonna be easy though," Emmett said.

"Nope. Never is," Delbert said.

They both sipped a little more whiskey. Their moods darkened a bit, both men contemplating the drive to come. The night before a drive always brought a sort of anxiousness. It was the night when the men, even hard men like Emmett and Delbert, doubted the wisdom of the path they'd chosen. They wondered if they'd live to the end of the drive. Once the drive was underway, there was precious little time to worry about such things, what with the constant vigilance required to keep the herd moving. Sure there'd be downtime and periods of boredom, but the knife's edge that all the men on the drive lived on kept a persistent sense of foreboding in the back, if not the front, of each of their minds.

"Anybody else I know coming along?" Delbert asked.

"Javier is coming," Emmett replied.

"That makes me feel better. He's as good a scout as I've ever seen," Delbert said. He thought how much he missed him since the end of the last drive. Spending months on the trail with the same group of men, facing challenging and dangerous conditions, forged deep bonds between them. Javier and Delbert's friendship was a perfect example of that.

"Deacon is still with us. He wintered at the Bar Nothin'", Emmett added. Delbert nodded his approval.

"Mighty good hand. Look forward to seeing him again," Delbert said.

"Mostly familiar faces. A few new ones. One is real new," Emmett said.

"What do you mean?" Delbert asked.

Emmett's thoughts turned to Ben. It's a hard thing, growing up in the modern world and in a big city like St. Louis. The rapid pace of change was hard for a man like him to contemplate, but Ben would become a grown man in a world of affordable, rapid transportation and communication. The ability to travel quickly on trains, and communicate via telegram had already made the country feel much smaller than when had he'd come of age. Of course the war had made everything feel different now.

Emmett's sister had married well enough, not rich, but to a good man who looked after his family. She'd borne him two sons and a daughter. Ben's younger brother had been run over by a runaway horse on a thoroughfare near their home and died when he was four. His younger sister was afflicted with a malady of the mind, "touched in the head" as the saying went. Emmett's sister never wrote much about the girl in her letters, other than to say that looking after her was no easy thing.

"My sister talked me into letting her son, my nephew Ben, come with us. Said he needs to finish becoming a man," Emmett said.

"You say that like I ain't gonna like what comes next," Delbert said.

"They lost my brother-in-law to a fever about a year and half ago. Ben's a smart kid, real smart. Works hard, too. Takes good care of my sister. He's a real good boy. It's just…" Emmett pauses, thinking of a way to downplay how green Ben really is. "He's never been on the trail before."

"Oh," Delbert said, comprehending the added work and the uncomfortable situation this created for Emmett, and the other boys.

The sun was just up as Deacon poured himself some more coffee. He offered some to Delbert and to Emmett, both of whom held out their cups to him. He filled those as well.

This being the final day before the drive would depart and head north, Deacon figured it would be the last morning in quite a long time that he would have breakfast in the daylight. In fact, it felt a bit of a luxury to start the breakfast fire when he could see his way around. Still, Deacon was glad the cosinero was coming today, and that he would be relieved of his duties as breakfast cook. Hucks was a much better cook than he, Deacon thought, but he was sure going to miss the suppers that Mrs. Callaway had sent out to them while they were getting ready to depart.

"When's Hucks coming in? I'm hungry enough to eat my saddle bags," asked Delbert. "No offense, Deacon, but there's only so much bacon and beans a man can eat for breakfast."

Deacon just smiled and nodded. "Believe me, I'm as anxious as you to see him." Then he laughed. "Ain't that a powerful bad thing for a man to hate his own cookin'?" He poked the fire to liven it up a bit.

"Well no man can be good at everything," Delbert said.

"Hopefully Huck's will be here in time for the mid-day chuck," Emmett said, then took another sip of coffee. "I do like your coffee better than his, I have to admit."

"It's the sand," Deacon said.

"The what?" Emmett asked.

"He's just funning you," Delbert said.

"No I ain't," Deacon replied with a grin. "Little something I learned from the Cheyenne when I was with the 10th."

"Do tell," Emmett said.

"Yessir. Got a tiny bit of sweet in it. You just sprinkle a pinch of sand in the coffee and it takes most of the bitter out of it."

"Well I'll be," Emmett said.

"But you gotta let it settle, like you do the grounds,

or else you…" Deacon said before being interrupted by Delbert.

"Who is that?" Delbert said, looking out into the distance as he stood up. "Is that Luke?"

Emmett and Deacon rose as well and looked toward the three riders approaching from the north.

"Sure looks like him," Deacon said.

"Yep. That'd be him, along with my nephew that I told you about, Delbert," Emmett said.

"Who's the third man?" Delbert asked.

"A new boy. Name's Johnny," Emmett said. "Now you rest easy, Deacon," he said, turning to look him in the eye.

"What do you mean?" Deacon asked.

"He wore gray."

Deacon doesn't try to hide his look of disapproval. "Johnny," he said then paused. "Surname o' Reb?" he said with a measure of sarcasm in his voice. Delbert let out a small laugh, then regretted it as he looked at Emmett.

The three riders approached and as they drew close, Luke called out, "Mornin' gents."

Luke was a young cowboy who, despite his age, had quite a few drives under his belt. He was well known for being a good hand on the trail, and particularly handy with a rope. He was equally well known as being a terrible gambler, short tempered, and bad at holding his liquor.

Johnny was an embittered veteran of the Civil War, taller than a typical cowboy, but lean and lanky. He had a nasty scar across one cheek and a slightly lazy eye, both the result of a bullet at close range during the Battle of Honey Springs in the Indian territory of Oklahoma. White soldiers were in the minority during that battle, with mostly

Indians fighting for the Confederate forces, and black soldiers fighting for the United States forces. The rout of the Confederate forces there, and the humiliation of having to leave their dead and wounded behind as they retreated, was still a source of deep contention and bitterness, even after nearly twenty years.

As Luke, Johnny, and Ben dismounted, Johnny seemed quite displeased with Deacon's presence.

"Welcome, Luke. Johnny," Emmett said. "Luke, you remember Delbert and Deacon, don't you?"

"Of course I do, Emmett," Luke said.

"Much obliged for you two getting' my nephew here in one piece," Emmett said to Luke and Johnny.

Emmett sized up Ben for a brief moment. "Good to see you, Ben. Your mother is well?"

"Yes, sir. She is well and grateful for you taking me along to Abilene, as am I," Ben said.

"Boys, this is John Robert," Emmett said to Delbert and Deacon again. "Johnny, Delbert and Deacon."

"Folks call me Johnny," he said, as they all shook hands, with the exception of Johnny and Deacon.

"Johnny Reb," Deacon muttered.

"How'd you get a fly in the sugar bowl?" Johnny said to Emmett. Deacon and Johnny both stiffened, eyeing each other warily and with much contempt.

"Now you boys shake hands. You both ride for the Bar Nothin' now and you'd do well to remember that," Emmett said to Johnny and Deacon. They reluctantly shook hands, each acting as if the other had an infectious disease of some sort.

Delbert felt obliged to make an attempt to lighten the mood.

"How ya been, Luke? That a new saddle?"

"Well new to me. Lost my good one over in Wichita Falls," Luke said.

"When you gonna learn that poker ain't your strong suit?" Delbert replied.

Luke just shrugged, not having any words to provide as reasonable defense.

As Deacon shook Ben's hand, he said, "Name's Deacon, Ben. You stick close to me. I'll look after you."

"Thank you, Deacon. I'll try my best not to burden the drive," Ben said.

"You won't be much help when we're moving anyhow, Deacon. I'll be keeping you on point most of the time. Gonna need you to keep 'em headed north," Emmett said.

"That's sounds just fine by me, Emmett. I've e't my fair share of dust ridin' drag over the years," Deacon replied.

In the distance, another rider approached.

Delbert knew him at a glance. "That'd be Javier coming," he said as he sat down and poured himself some more coffee. The others joined him, sitting down by the fire.

"You boys help yourself to some breakfast," Emmett said to the three new arrivals.

Javier looked toward the camp as he drew nearer, recognizing some of the figures gathered around the small cooking fire. He instantly picked out his old friend, Delbert. And the trail boss, Emmett. And Deacon of course. His keen eyes could only recognize one of the other three seated by the fire, though his name escaped Javier. He did remember that the man was often quite disagreeable.

Javier arrived in camp and dismounted, tying the reins of his horse's bridle loosely to the makeshift hitching post where several other horses were tied, saddled and at the ready.

"Boys, this is Javier Rodriguez. The best scout in the great state of Texas," Emmett announced.

"Well, it's nice to see you too, Emmett. With that introduction, they'll be expecting me to walk across the Red River on foot when we get to her," Javier replied, not accustomed to the spotlight. After years of scouting on numerous cattle trails, he had grown used to the solitude. It was a lonely business, going for days without seeing another human being, his only companion being the horse beneath him. It was during those times when he found it so easy to dream of his Rosa. Even his active imagination, though, wasn't equal to the task of magnifying her true beauty.

"Javier, it's great to see you. How is Rosa?" Delbert said.

"She is well. She is looking after our remuda with Ellie."

"Ellie? That Adam's young wife?"

Javier nodded in the affirmative, apparently not wanting to say what was left unsaid.

"Shame the end he met," Delbert said, after a pause that felt longer than it was.

"Yes, Adam's widow. She has a fine young son. Adam didn't know of him," Javier said in a softer voice.

Ben looked very confused and turned to Emmett as if to ask for an explanation.

"Adam was a drover on last year's drive. His horse got bogged in a crossing and he drowned. We buried him just north of Sherman," Emmett said to Ben, who nodded with comprehension, a sadness creeping over his face.

"Still just you and Rosa?" Delbert asked Javier.

"Yes." Delbert and Javier share a look of mutual understanding. Still no child. Still no son.

"Any news?" Emmett asked Javier.

"There's a herd three or four days ahead. Moving well but not leaving much behind for us," Javier replied.

"Well if there's a drive behind us, they'll have it rough. With our size we won't be leaving much at all for them, unless the weather breaks soon," Emmett said.

"We've got a good two days before the first crossing," Javier said. "How many head are we?"

"We'll do a full count after the mid-day meal, but I'd bet around forty five hundred based on my rough count," Emmett answered. "Between the range cows we'll pick up and calves that'll be borned on the way, we might be upwards of five thousand come the end."

"That's quite a herd. At least to start," Javier said. He looked at Emmett with a measure of seriousness that gave even more weight to his words. "Emmett, I fear a very dry trip," he said.

Emmett nodded and paused before replying.

"Gonna be a hard trail. That we can believe."

Emmett poured himself some more coffee and took a worried sip. He pulled out his constant companion, his dog eared notebook, from his shirt pocket along with a short marker and began jotting down some more notes.

Johnny and Deacon were sitting across the fire from one another. It would have been clear to even the most casual observer that each man's dislike for the other was rooted in something much deeper, much older, and much stronger than them. Each man stared across the fire at the other, Johnny in particular seeking to assert his dominance but cautious about Emmett seeing his antagonistic demeanor. Deacon, for his part, just stared coldly at Johnny, undaunted, his gaze devoid of fear or emotion. He'd seen men like this before, hard men, shaped by experience and driven by hatred sourced from a well poisoned by the mores of a culture that hated change more than it hated men like Deacon. He also knew well enough to hold his ground with a man like Johnny, if there was to be any chance of breaking past the barrier between them. In fact, it was his way, the only way he knew to be.

The quiet of the little camp was abruptly shattered by a commotion as Hucks McPherson approached in the drive's chuck wagon. It was pulled by two mules, both strong and steady, but exceedingly motley in appearance. The same could be said for Hucks, in fact. He was stout, heavyset man in his fifties, or maybe in his seventies, no one was really sure and no one really wanted to ask. Just as no one dared ask about his poor excuse for a hat. It was a wide, somewhat floppy brimmed number that was something of a cross between the traditional hat of cowboys and a sombrero that a salty old hombre from Guadalajara might wear. The years and the miles were evidenced by the sweat-stained headband. The scraggly gray hair that flowed from under that old hat was longer than most wore it. The ravages of the bottle over the years had taken their toll, as had the years on the trail. Cantankerous by nature, worsened by age and hard times, he was the sort that a drive needed to keep the boys fed and working, with a minimum of fuss and foolishness.

The men all stood up from their places around the fading cook fire.

"Emmett! These have got to be the worst two mules the Good Lord ever put on this earth," Hucks called out. "I've seen porch dogs with more git up and go. What'd you give for these things? A passel of last year's jerky?"

Emmett couldn't help but laugh out loud.

"Well it's about time, Hucks. Got a hungry bunch needing their mid-day meal and wondering if you'd ever get here," he said. "I trust you weren't delayed by spending time with the spirits," he said, this time with a tone of gravity.

"No sir. The Dry Goods was awful busy and layin' in supplies took a might longer than I figured on."

"Well I'm glad you got here. Let's get these boys fed so we can get our final count this afternoon, before dark. We'll head north at first light," he said. "Deacon and young Ben here laid up some wood for you."

"Much obliged, Deacon," Hucks said. "Howdy, Delbert."

"Good to see ya, Hucks," Delbert answered.

"Well don't just stand there takin' up space. Help me get my stove set up, so I can get you fed," Hucks said, to no one in particular.

With the boys' help, Hucks started unloading his wagon.

"As soon as Hucks gets the chuck ready, you boys eat quick and then move out and relieve the swing men so they can come eat. I want to be counting cattle in two hours," Emmett said to the men.

CHAPTER FIVE

HEADING NORTH

THE COUNT COMMENCED IMMEDIATELY AFTER the men had eaten their mid-day meal, consisting of biscuits, beans and coffee. These foods that would serve as staples for most meals on the drive with the addition of some bacon at breakfast and beef at dinner.

Having an accurate accounting of the size of the herd, along with a rough categorization of the beeves according to size and weight, was critical to the financial success of the drive. The trail boss needed to know what he was starting with, so that adjusting for estimates of strays lost, calves born on the way, and range cattle that joined the herd as they went, he'd have a good idea of what the size of the herd would be once they reached their destination, Abilene, Kansas. None had a better reputation amongst the big Texas ranchers for detail and accuracy than Emmett Logan.

The count was long, slow, and tedious work, but then again, just about everything associated with these trail drives was long, slow, and tedious. Hour by hour, a group of the men gathered small bunches of cattle together, perhaps a few dozen at a time, squeezing them through a narrow gate built just for the purpose of the day's work. Emmett, along with Delbert as El Segundo, counted the cattle as they passed through, then compared their results to one another as the next bunch was being gathered. Once each bunch passed through to the other side of the gate, the rest of the men kept the cattle who had been counted segregated from those not yet counted.

It was dusk when the count was finally complete. As usual, Emmett's rough estimate was close but a bit conservative, the final count coming in at just a tad over five thousand — five thousand one hundred and seventeen to be exact. This fact was duly recorded in Emmett's logbook. That information, along with other details of the drive, such as the rough mix of cows and steers, number of horses in the remuda, and the like, was also shared with Mr. Callaway by way of Jip. Emmett sent him to the Big House carrying a letter containing the final particulars of the journey that would begin at first light the next day.

The men, with the exception of the first night shift, sat around the small fire Hucks had made for them. Separate from his cook fire which was bigger and hotter, this smaller fire was what Hucks referred to as his coffee fire, over which the coffee was kept hot. It also served as a place for the men to gather for meals and an area to bed down for the few hours of sleep they would get each night. It wasn't foolproof but it *did* help keep the snakes away at night, for the most part.

Dinner consisted of beans and biscuits with some fresh beef, but with the pleasant addition of pecan pies, a half dozen of which were sent out to the men from Mrs. Callaway, her gesture of goodwill and good wishes for the drive. The men relaxed and drank coffee after their meal, as Hucks cleaned and packed his cookware in preparation for the next morning. Ben, for his part, had eaten and enjoyed the basic meal, but was very much struggling with the coffee. *Too hot and too strong*, he thought. But he persevered and made the best of it. He knew it was something he'd have to get used to.

The cattle were bedded down, lowing quietly, as Emmett returned to the camp after stepping away to relieve himself. He settled by the small fire and poured himself some coffee.

"Well men, it's a long way to Abilene," Emmett said. "Delbert, did you get the night shift sorted out?"

"Yes sir, I did," Delbert said. "I spared young Ben the graveyard shift tonight, but I'll make sure he gets an extra to make up for it somewhere up the trail." He grinned at Ben, who wasn't sure if he ought to be grateful for the reprieve or concerned about the extra shift.

"Good," Emmett replied. "You men get your rest. Spivey will have your mounts ready before daybreak," he said.

With that, he laid back against his saddle, pulled his hat down over his eyes, and said a quick and quiet prayer asking the Lord for a safe drive for the men, the horses, and the cattle.

Ben emulated his uncle's movements but took a good while to get settled, not yet being accustomed to sleeping on the ground. After tossing and turning and squirming his way around a troublesome object for several painful minutes, he finally reached under his bedroll and found the rock, which was about the size of a pecan and had been keeping his rest from him. *That's better*, he thought. After that, the ground under him felt strangely comforting and he felt the sleep coming on easily. As Ben pulled his hat down over his eyes, Emmett was already snoring.

The morning started before the night was over, or so it seemed to Ben, when Hucks rang his bell announcing breakfast. He'd slept a fitful sleep, and woke up sore from the ground, but excited nonetheless. It was still dark, but off to the east, the first rays of sun were cautiously peeking over the horizon. The air was still cool, yet a bit more humid than the day before, a sure sign of a warm day ahead.

"Get up and eat, you lazy bunch o' yard birds!" Hucks said loudly enough to achieve his purpose of rousing the slower movers, among whom Ben was not. "This ain't Sunday mornin'."

This being the first day of the drive, Hucks had yet another treat for the boys, once again courtesy of Mrs. Callaway. She seemed to love the men who worked for her husband, but only when they were not around. Food from the ranch house was her way of caring for them in the best manner she could manage.

"You boys better enjoy them eggs. Mrs. Callaway sent 'em out special for you from her coops, and they'll likely be the last you'll see 'fore we hit Abilene. Maybe I'll get lucky and run across a covey or two of quail on the trail, but we'll see nary a chicken, so eat up."

Ben fumbled to fill his plate in the darkness of the very early morning and tripped over the stirrup of one of the men's saddles that were strewn about. He found his way back to his own saddle and leaned against it as he sat down on the ground. Ben ate his breakfast quickly, as did the other men, even managing to down a little of the piping hot coffee in the process. Quite an accomplishment, he thought, especially managing to hide the effort required to keep a straight face as he sipped.

Not wanting to unwittingly give them any reminders of how green he was, Ben mirrored the actions of the other men after breakfast was done, and did as they did to the best of his ability. He picked up his saddle and followed them to the makeshift picket line where Spivey had tied the horses.

The morning light was beginning to crowd out the darkness and Ben could see just well enough to tell one horse from another. Spivey was having a bit of a rough time settling one of the horses, a big grey gelding, when he noticed that Ben was near.

"This one here is yours for the day," Spivey said to Ben, putting his hand on the neck of the horse, who shuddered nervously at the touch. Ben nodded and stepped toward the horse, taking the lead rope from Spivey. He was disconcerted and quite worried that the horse might be too skittish to handle, but he was determined not to let Spivey, or anyone else, see his fear. Deacon was standing next to Ben and took notice, giving Spivey a look of disapproval. *He ought to know better*, Deacon thought.

"Why don't we let him ride Banjo today?" Deacon said to Spivey, matter-of-factly. "I'll ride the grey."

Spivey nodded, as a look of understanding crossed his face. "Suit yourself." The exchange gave Spivey a new worry as it sunk in just how green Ben was. Each man on the drive usually had six horses that were his mounts for the drive.

They would change horses two or three times a day, and rest each horse every other day. Conserving their mounts was a critical component of the cowboys' responsibility on the trail. Spivey wondered if Ben's lack of experience would cause him to go through more than his share of the remuda, making it all the more difficult for the more experienced men to make it to the end of the drive.

Deacon pointed to the sorrel horse next to the grey and said to Ben, "This here is Banjo. He's one of my favorites. Y'all will get along just fine." Deacon handed Ben the bridle that he had been about to put on Banjo. Ben put his saddle on the ground and, with some difficulty, put the bridle on his mount.

"Good boy. Now saddle up and let's get going," Deacon said, encouraged by the boy's apparent willingness and ability to learn the ropes.

Hucks packed and loaded the chuck wagon after the morning meal, then headed north ahead of the drive. He needed to put at least an hour, if not two, between himself and the herd in order to have enough time to prepare the mid-day meal for the men, so they would not have to wait to eat. He would do the same in advance of the evening meal, and the same most every day of the drive. Normally, staying ahead wouldn't be a great challenge given that the herd would usually only travel twelve to fifteen miles in a typical day. With the herd for this drive being so large, progress would likely be even slower, so barring any trouble with the wagon or difficulties in scouting wood for the cook fire, Hucks felt good about how things were shaping up. He was in high spirits. In fact, his spirits were so high, he even spoke kindly to the mules as they trudged along, singing to them from time to time, which was not a usual thing for him at all.

The men, once mounted, gathered around Emmett who was also horseback, as was Javier who was next to him.

"Deacon, you're on point like we talked about," he said, direct as ever. "See if a lead steer don't identify himself before the day is out. You other boys keep your eyes open for one too." Deacon nodded, acknowledging the fact that it made the drive go much more smoothly if one of the steers, it was always a steer, led the herd north, unafraid to look ahead and not see other cattle in front of him.

"Delbert, you and Johnny take the swing. Luke, you and Ben start out on the drag. Hector and Red will go with you. The rest of you boys will be on the swing with Delbert," he continued. Luke didn't even try to hide his dissatisfaction. Ben looked puzzled.

"What's a drag?" Ben asked Luke.

"Get ready to eat dust," Luke replied.

"It means you're bringing up the rear, and pushing the herd forward," Emmett said, answering more directly. "Delbert will swap you boys around after a while if I ain't back. I'm going to scout with Javier and hopefully be back to meet the drive by supper tomorrow night. While I'm gone, Delbert is in charge. He's El Segundo and you answer to him until I get back."

Emmett looked around at the men, making sure he had their attention and that they'd been listening.

Johnny caught Emmett's gaze and gestured toward

Deacon. "I'm gonna have to follow him all the way to Abilene?" he said with a measure of sourness in his tone.

This set Delbert off, not taking kindly to the barb directed at his friend. "You'll follow him to hell if that's where the drive heads," Delbert said.

"Delbert, you don't have to speak for me," Deacon replied.

"And besides, if you…" Delbert said before being interrupted.

"Delbert, that's enough," Emmett said.

He turned to Johnny with a look that would wither the will of most men. "I warned you before and I don't like to repeat myself. You ride for the brand, and if you can't see yourself doing that, then now'd be a good time to draw your wages and head back to town."

"I didn't mean no harm," Johnny said in an inauthentic attempt to defuse the situation, though the fleeting glance he cast in the direction of Deacon would have suggested otherwise.

"Let's go," Delbert said, his voice dripping with disgust.

Delbert turned his horse toward the north and kicked his mount into a slow trot, glancing over his shoulder to make sure Johnny was following, which he was. They reached the edge of the herd, but Johnny kept his distance from Delbert, not wanting to engage him further.

"Ben, go with Luke and mind what he tells you," Emmett said.

"Yes, sir," Ben replied eagerly.

Luke tied his bandana over his nose and mouth. Ben regretted not having one to put into service for himself. Emmett, being a step ahead of matters, reached into his saddlebag and pulled out a new, neatly folded bandana, handing it over to his nephew.

"Thought you might could use this," Emmett said.

"Thank you, Uncle Emmett, er... I mean, Emmett," Ben said as he unfolded the bandana. He looked at Luke and attempted to emulate the manner he had tied it so it would stay put.

"Come on, kid," Luke said, wheeling his mount toward the back of the herd. Ben followed, excited and eager for the adventure to begin.

"Deacon, head 'em up. It's time," Emmett said, his voice booming so all the men could hear.

"Yes, sir," Deacon replied with a slight, but noticeable level of excitement in his voice.

Emmett and Javier pointed their horses north, kicking them into an easy canter as they rode off to scout ahead of the herd.

The boys slowly got the herd organized and some of the steers headed north, with Deacon on point. At first the herd just seemed to be milling aimlessly, but slowly, over the course of fifteen or twenty minutes, they began to move in the same general direction. It was a couple of hours before the swing riders were able to narrow up the column sufficiently for the herd to make noticeable progress.

By the time the sun was high in the sky, the herd was making good time, and it was getting quite warm.

CHAPTER SIX

HELLO AND GOODBYE

J AVIER AND EMMETT RODE ALL morning, varying the speed and gate of their horses to save them for the journey, sometimes an easy canter, sometimes a slow trot, sometimes just a walk. High above them, a trio of buzzards circled slowly, scanning about unsuccessfully for a carcass to hold their interest. The two men had pulled their horses back to a brisk walk, fast enough to still be covering ground at a decent pace, but also slow enough to not overly task them in the warm sun. Javier looked up and noticed that the sun had reached its zenith. It was near mid-day. He also took notice of the buzzards above, as did Emmett.

"They must have fed within the last couple of days, or they wouldn't still be around," Javier said.

"Sure enough. Nothing close by for them it seems. Elsewise, they'd be flying a good bit closer to the ground," Emmett replied.

"Si," Javier agreed. He squinted and looked in the distance to the north. "There's water ahead."

"I swear you've got better eyes than them buzzards up there," Emmett said with a grin.

"A blessing I'm sure," Javier said.

He kicked his horse into a trot, and Emmett did likewise.

It took about twenty minutes to reach the creek that Javier had spotted, and they slowed their horses as they approached it. They dismounted and gave their horses a drink and a rest. Both men also drank and topped of their canteens, which were hanging from their saddles. As the horses drank and stood knee deep in the cool water, Javier studied the ground, slowly walking up and down the creek, then away from it a few hundred feet, then back to its bank.

"A drive crossed here four, maybe five days ago," Javier said, pausing to look upstream. "Creek was much higher then, too."

"Water's running mighty slow, too," Emmett said, motioning downstream. "Wouldn't surprise me if it peters out not too far down that way."

"Could be," Javier said.

Emmett gathered his horse and mounted up. "We should get moving."

Javier mounted his horse as well.

"I think I'll ride west, upstream, and follow it for a spell. See if I can tell what's feeding it," Emmett said. "Why don't you ride north and look for next water?"

"All right. I'll figure on being back with the drive in two days. The herd should make it this far by then," Javier said.

"Should be if we don't have weather."

Emmett gave Javier's horse a thorough looking over.

"Go easy on that mare now. This is mighty bad country to be sore footin' it," Emmett said.

Javier grinned widely, his bright smile obscured only by one slightly discolored front tooth, deadened by a colt's hoof when he was seventeen. He was, and remained grateful that it was merely a glancing blow. Otherwise, he feared, his Rosa would have waited for a more pleasant looking husband.

"She'll be fine. She's Commanche bred," he said, patting her on the neck. "I've never had a horse that could travel so far on so little."

"They do come that way. It's true," Emmett said. "All the same, mind your pace anyhow."

"Si, I will. See you in two days."

Javier turned north and crossed the creek, moving at a steady, patient pace. Emmett crossed the creek as well, then headed west along the north bank of the creek. He looked up and smiled. No sign of the buzzards.

The rest of the first day had gone uneventfully. The drive had made good time, and Delbert was sure that Emmett would be pleased with their progress. The night also had passed without incident, although the graveyard shift, which ran from midnight until dawn, had caused Delbert some worry. He'd assigned Ben to join a couple of the other boys. They reported back that Ben had stayed alert and engaged the entire shift. He looked forward to informing Emmett of how Ben had, not only pulled his first overnight shift, but had done so in an exemplary fashion. Ben was certainly green, but Delbert was really starting to like him, and saw that he was cut from the same cloth as his uncle, who was a man they both admired very much.

The next morning, after the early morning meal, the drive was on its way again. Deacon on point, and quite happy that he'd not only found a lead steer that had no fear of walking ahead of the herd, but one that was stout and hardy. By Deacon's reckoning, he surely weighed at least eighteen hundred pounds, with a set of horns that must have been as wide, point to point, as he was tall.

The morning progressed and the sun was getting high in the sky. It wasn't yet mid-day and Deacon rode back to the remuda. On the ground in the middle of the horses, Spivey, the reins of his horse clutched in one hand, sat shivering in the hot sun.

"Spivey, I need to swap mounts. This horse is spent," Deacon said as he approached the remuda, at first not noticing Spivey on the ground. "What'n the heck's got into you?"

"Snakebit," Spivey muttered through teeth gritted in an attempt to ward off their chattering.

"Mother of Texas! What happened?" Deacon quickly dismounted, leaving his horse to mingle with the others, and went to Spivey.

"I was hobbling one of the horses and the son of a gun got the jump on me. Never even rattled. Horse didn't even see it 'til he bit me."

"Let me go for help," Deacon said.

Spivey looked at Deacon for a long moment. "No need. I'm done for," he said.

"Dear Lord." Deacon hesitated, watching another uncontrollable shiver take claim of Spivey's body. There was no point going for help. He'd just be leaving his friend to die alone.

"Deacon, will you do something for me?"

"If I can, you know I will," Deacon responded.

He rolled up the sleeve of Spivey's shirt, and saw that it was swollen and distended. Deacon had no doubt that Spivey was beyond help.

"Take a good account of where you bury me." Spivey could barely speak he was shaking so hard. "Get a letter to my sister in Austin, so she can send for my bones and bring 'em home."

Deacon removed his hat.

"She'll want to have me close to home, by and by."

Taking the reins of his horse that Spivey had been clutching so tightly, Deacon got up and retrieved the man's canteen, offering it to him. Spivey drank a little but couldn't manage much. Deacon stayed with him, comforting him as best he could, but it didn't take long for Spivey to pass. As he slung Spivey's body across his saddle, Deacon sighed heavily, thinking how fragile life was, particularly on the trail. He wondered who but Spivey's sister would truly remember him. The men he rode with would speak of him from time to time, but his memory would fade from their own before long.

A couple of hours later, after the men had gathered, and Delbert and Deacon had said some words, the drive was moving on. As they left behind the shallow grave and makeshift marker, most of the men cast a lingering glance backward, saying goodbye to Spivey, each in his own way.

The rest of the day saw good progress, with the herd moving further on its journey. But the loss of Spivey weighed heavily on the men and the evening meal was somber and subdued. Afterward, as the men not on night watch were gathered around the fire, Delbert had proposed a game of poker. Ben was still new to the game, but willing to give it a go. The quiet sound of the cattle lowing provided a soft, but constant backdrop.

Delbert shuffled the deck of cards he kept tucked away, safely dry in Hucks' chuck wagon, and dealt another hand to himself, Luke, Johnny and Ben. As the betting went around, it was clear that Ben had not been dealt a hand worth playing.

"I'm not sure I'll ever get the hang of this game. I fold," Ben said, somewhat dejected as he lay his cards down.

"You've been playing for a few days now, Ben. You ought to give yourself a bit more time," Delbert said.

"Ahh, I'll take his money and not lose a wink over it," Luke said, a touch of glee in his voice.

"Best I can tell, you don't lose many winks over much. Took me forever to wake you for your watch last night," Johnny added.

"I was deep dreaming about all that money I'm gonna bring home from Abilene, once we get there," Luke said.

"My advice would be to leave your saddle and your pistol in the Marshall's office. Ya know, for safe keeping and all," Delbert said.

"I only ever lost one saddle in a poker game and never a pistol," Luke replied.

"That's only 'cause I "bought" it from you so you could settle with them fellas in Laredo," Delbert said. He looked down at Luke's Peacemaker. "How is my pistol anyhow? Taking good care of it for me?" he said, chiding Luke.

Hucks, who had been listening to the conversation,

while cleaning up after the dinner meal, said "You hens do more cackling than playing cards."

A faint but unmistakable sound of rustling grass and a snapped twig put them all instantly on alert. The silhouette of a small rider on a similarly proportioned horse appeared in the light of the campfire.

"Howdy," a small voice said. It was Joe, slumped in his saddle, his brown pony slowly walked closer to the camp.

Instinctively, the men jumped to their feet and drew their weapons.

"That's a good way to get blown all to pieces," Johnny said, more annoyed than the others.

Once the men got a good look at Joe, they relaxed and put away their guns. The boy was very weak and fainted, slipping from his saddle. His pony, aging and big hearted, stopped when he felt Joe start to come down. Delbert was closest to him and was able to catch him before he hit the ground. He carried Joe's frail figure near the fire and gently laid him down. Deacon took the reins of the pony and led him away, tying the reins to a mesquite tree.

After a few moments, the boy came to, disoriented but able to sip from the canteen Delbert pressed to his lips. This revived Joe a little and he looked around at the faces of the men looking at him, none very sure what to make of him.

"I'm gonna venture that you're mighty hungry, son," Delbert said.

"Yes, sir."

"Hucks, get him some grub," Delbert said in a calm but firm voice.

Hucks, still cleaning up after the dinner meal,

grumbled under his breath, "Sure, sure, make more work for ol' Hucks."

"Have you traveled far?" Delbert said to Joe.

"I'm not really sure."

"When did you eat last?"

"Well, I squirreled away a little cornbread right before I left. I think it was Sunday. I saw folks headed to town for church." He paused for a moment. "My Stepma never let me go to church, but I wanted to." He paused again. "What day is it?"

The men all looked around, exchanging glances with each other, and then back to Joe, some perplexed, some with pity.

"It's Thursday, Joe," Delbert said.

It had been a wearying couple of days for Emmett scouting to the north. But, he was pleased at how far the drive had progressed by the time he made it back to meet them. He came upon camp much sooner than he expected. As he neared, he signaled his arrival, hopeful that Hucks had some chuck left for him.

"Comin' into camp, boys," Emmett announced loudly, so as not to startle the camp by his arrival.

Hucks served Joe a plate of food, his demeanor considerably less than friendly. Joe began eating with abandon.

"Who's this little feller?" Emmett asked.

"This here's Joe, Emmett. He's a stray that wandered into camp from somewhere east of here," Delbert answered.

"Is that right?" Emmett said. He watched Joe for a moment as he furiously attacked the plate of food. "How old are you son?" he asked.

Joe interrupted his eating and swallowed the oversized mouthful of beans. "Not sure, sir."

"What do you mean you're not sure?"

"I don't know," Joe replied, pausing to think. "Ten, maybe eleven."

"What year were you born?"

"I don't know, sir. Nobody ever told me."

Emmett reflected on the situation for a moment, then said to Delbert, "Well after he eats, bed him down and come daybreak, send him back."

Joe resumed eating, scraping the last of the food from his plate. Hucks took the plate from him and went off to refill it, seeing that Joe was clearly still quite hungry.

"Well... I ain't so sure that's a good idea. His Pa's gone and all he's got is a stepma that beats him every day or two," Delbert said. "Besides, he's been wanderin' since Sunday so I ain't sure he'd know his way back anyhow."

Emmett looked for another long moment at Joe.

"Sir, I'm very grateful for the meal. He's right. I runned off and I can't go back there. She'd beat me to death if I go back," Joe said to Emmett, who was visibly unconvinced.

"I don't know much about cattle, 'cept milkin' the ones back home. But I do know a lot about hard work. If you'll let me stay on, I promise I'll earn my keep and won't be no bother," Joe said.

Emmett was just about to respond in the negative, thinking of Ben being on the drive and not wanting to have another green kid for the men to have to look after.

"Emmett, there's another thing you need to know. We're without a proper Wrangler now," Delbert said.

"What? Where's Spivey?"

"Snakebit. We had to bury him a half a day back," Delbert replied.

Emmett lowered his gaze to the ground and muttered to himself, "Too soon for poor luck." He just stood there for an uncomfortably long minute, eyes on the ground, uncharacteristically indecisive. The men took note of that, but no one knew quite what to say, not even Delbert, so they all stood there too, waiting for Emmett to speak.

Emmett looked up and then to Joe. "Tell you what. If you'll work hard and help Hucks with the chuck, and learn to wrangle the remuda proper, I'll let you stay on," he said. "Delbert here is El Segundo, second in charge. He'll teach you. Mind what Hucks says and don't give him no sass. He's a might prickly."

Hucks had made a plate of food for Emmett, knowing that he would be hungry. He'd heard the conversation and the mention of his name. "Sure, make me a wet nurse for ever' little mongrel that comes into camp," he grumbled as he handed Emmett his supper.

"Try to tolerate the boy, Hucks. If he ain't pulling his weight, we'll leave him off in Fort Worth," Emmett said as he sat down and began to eat. "Delbert, you have the night shift settled in?"

"Yes, sir," Delbert answered.

"Good," Emmett said. "Bed the boy down and let him get some sleep. He looks like he ain't slept in a while," he said, motioning in Joe's direction.

CHAPTER SEVEN

THE ROPES

THE GRAVEYARD SHIFT RETURNED TO camp at the nexus between night and morning. Hucks had already awoken, but not yet stirred, enjoying the last few minutes to himself in the quiet stillness of the camp. To him, it was the best part of the day, a time when no one wanted anything from him, no one needed him to be working on something, nothing to prepare for or to clean up after. Just stillness while most of the cattle were still sleeping. That morning, his thoughts were troubled by the arrival of the stray the night before. It's not like he had anything against the boy. He just knew that having him along on the drive meant another to worry about, kept fed, looked after. The boy was another pain in his backside, which he neither needed nor wanted. The drive was hard enough on everyone already. Most of all, he resented Joe's intrusion into the quiet of his morning mind.

Hucks tossed and turned for a few more minutes until his frustration got the better of him.

"Aw, hell," he said as he threw back his bedroll and began putting on his boots. He got dressed quickly as the eastern sky grew red. The first rays of sunlight would be creeping over the horizon all too soon, marking the beginning of another long and tedious day. He made his way to the nearly dead campfire, reviving it enough to illuminate the camp. The pot of coffee, hours old by now, was still warm but would soon be hot enough to make it almost palatable to drink. The men sleeping about began to stir, waking up reluctantly, still bone tired from the day before.

Delbert was the first to be dressed and ready, knowing that he had to get the horses ready for the men. He poured a cup of the rancid coffee and took a sip. Even being prepared for its foulness, he underestimated just how awful it would taste. "Hucks, this coffee would wake the dead."

Hucks didn't reply. He noticed in the dim light that Joe's bedroll was abandoned. The blanket was still there, but without Joe. He let out a self-satisfied grunt. "Runned off," he said. "Figgers. Give him a good meal and he skins out at first light."

He made his way back to his wagon, intent on getting a fresh pot of coffee going for the men. He was startled by Joe's sudden appearance in camp, carrying as much firewood as his spindly arms could manage. He slowly dropped the load onto a very substantial pile of wood stacked neatly at the edge of camp.

"Mornin', Mister Hucks, sir," Joe said quietly, unsure how loudly he should be talking with the camp only just coming to life. "I hope I didn't wake y'all. I was tryin' to stack as quiet as I could."

Hucks, caught by surprise at the unexpected turn of events, was quite conflicted. On the one hand, having been briefly pleased by the thought that he was shed of the extra work and worry Joe would bring. On the other hand, he had to admit the boy had some gumption.

"Well don't just stand there. Bring me some of the shorter pieces, so I can get this oven fire goin'. I've got men to feed."

Delbert and some of the other men, who'd woken up and observed the scene, shared a laugh at Hucks' expense. Joe was frozen for a moment, confused at the laughter of the men, but quickly began picking up wood until he had his arms full. Then he scurried over to the wagon with it, laying it beside the stove.

Joe was eager to please his new companions, though he believed firmly that the grumpy man they called Hucks would have it in for him. He wondered if he'd be beaten if he displeased the man. He wondered if Delbert or the trail boss, Mr. Logan would permit it, or if they would join in, or if they would even know. Would he be any better off traveling with these men than he would have been if he'd stayed home? His spirits sank and he began to retreat into the place in his mind where he always went to try to protect himself.

Joe was abruptly brought back to the moment by the gruff sound of Hucks' voice. "Take this coffee pot over and set it on the fire, over there by Delbert. Bring back the one that's there and hurry back." He quickly handed Joe the coffee pot. Joe nearly dropped it. "Careful!" Hucks admonished. Joe put both hands on the pot and carried it to the fire.

"Go easy there, Hucks," Delbert said. "He ain't your man servant. I aim to make a proper wrangler out of him and I can't have him steppin' and fetchin' for your all the time." He grinned at Hucks, who was trying to maintain his cantankerous attitude, which was starting to require too much energy.

There was something about Joe that Delbert liked. Though he was a pitifully thin and very poorly clothed, Joe seemed to not be bothered by it. Nor was there a shred of self-pity or shame on his part. Malnourishment and hard use were a part of a cowboy's life. It came with the job. Delbert had a feeling that Joe, being no stranger to either, would make a fine cowboy. What he didn't know, but intended to find out, was if Joe had any horse sense. That too was part of the life of a working cowboy. The horse under a cowboy was a partner, a savior, a work tool, and at times, even a friend. A man needed to know his mount and understand him, knowing when to rest him, when he could push him harder, sense if we was going lame before it was too late to save him. Delbert hoped that Joe had enough of the innate ability needed to take over the role of Wrangler. The drive needed the help. *He* needed the help.

As Joe was helping Hucks finish cleaning up after breakfast and loading his wagon to move on ahead for the mid-day meal, Delbert approached them, mounted on a stocky palomino, and leading a shortish chestnut gelding with a blazed face and one white sock.

"You ready to get to work, Joe?" Delbert asked.

"Yes, sir I…" Joe replied before being interrupted.

"What do you think he's been doin' this morning?" Hucks chimed in, annoyed.

"Don't get testy, Hucks. The day is too young and I've got too much to teach the boy," Delbert said.

Hucks was tying down a sack of flour on the back of his wagon. He grumbled and muttered something unintelligible under his breath, then noticed that Joe was still standing there. He waved him on with his hand. "Go on then. See to the horses," he said gruffly, but with a slight, imperceptible tenderness that neither Joe nor Delbert noticed.

"Come on, Joe. Mount up. We've got cowboyin' to do," Delbert said.

Joe took the reins and mounted the little gelding, settling into the saddle as he followed Delbert. He realized the stirrups were a bit too long, but didn't want to say anything for fear of angering Delbert. He was glad to be headed away from the orneriness of Hucks.

"Ride up next to me, Joe," Delbert said.

Joe gave his horse a little kick. The horse quickened his pace to catch up and in short order they were walking abreast of one another.

"Joe, do you know what a remuda is?" Delbert asked.

"No sir. I don't know the first thing about cattle drives, 'cept that it sure seems like a mighty big operation ," Joe replied.

"The remuda is the herd of horses that the cowboys on the drive ride."

Joe listened intently, eager to hear what Delbert had to say. He enjoyed being with the man who genuinely wanted to teach him.

"This is on the large size for a drive. We're about five thousand head, there are about a dozen drovers, plus the cosinero – that's Hucks, plus the trail boss – that's Emmett, er, Mr. Logan. There's also the wrangler. He's the one who tends the remuda and keeps the men mounted and able to work."

The pair approached the herd of horses that Deacon had hobbled the night before. Deacon had offered to help tend the horses until Joe had learned enough to look after them. Emmett had agreed to allow it, but only for a few days. Deacon was needed on point to keep the drive headed north at a solid pace.

"Most trail bosses take about six or so horses for each man on the drive. They'll go through two, three, or even four in a day, then give each a day of rest before using them again. Emmett is a very different kind of trail boss. He believes in taking more horses and insists that the owner of the cattle provide for extra mounts, eight or ten per man. Emmett also believes that the wrangler should be a grown man with experience, not a green kid like most trail bosses." He paused and was pleased to see how eager Joe was to hear his words.

"So our remuda is well over a hundred head, a hundred and nineteen last I counted."

"A hundred and twenty counting Chaw!" Joe added with a smile.

"Well I don't know about that, Joe. Your little brown pony won't be much good on the trail." He paused again, unsure of how to say what he needed to say. Joe's smile disappeared. "Your pony is pretty old and looks mighty poorly. We'll let him follow along the drive with the other horses, but I wouldn't count on him making it all the way to Abilene."

"I see," Joe said, desperately trying to hide his disappointment.

"But, then again," Delbert said. "It's easy to underestimate the size of a horse's heart. He surely might make it. Let's just take it one day at a time. Fair enough?"

"Yes, sir."

Delbert dismounted when they reached the remuda.

"Morning, Deacon," Delbert said.

"Morning," Deacon replied without looking up. He was busy taking the hobbles off the horses so they could begin to move along. They had to keep up with the cattle.

"We'll finish up with that," Delbert said. "You can go ahead and join the cattle."

"Much obliged," Deacon said.

"No, I'm much obliged to *you* for helping out with the remuda," Delbert said.

"Happy to do it, Delbert." Deacon looked at Joe, who had dismounted too. "Delbert here knows horses better'n about anyone I know. He'll school you right up and you'll be the full time wrangler lickety split. You listen good to him, alright?" he said, grinning widely.

"Yes sir, Mr. Deacon. I will," Joe replied. He looked at the rope hobbles wrapped loosely around the front legs of the horses, sitting just atop the hooves. "What are those for?" he asked.

"Those are called hobbles. We use them to keep the horses from wandering too far at night. They can graze and walk around a bit, but they can't run off. Makes 'em easier to gather in the mornings," Delbert said. "Let's get busy getting these off the horses so they can be on their way, and so can we. It's going to be a long day and there's much to do." He turned away for a moment, "Thanks again, Deacon."

Deacon nodded and mounted his own horse, then turned to join the other men, kicking the horse into a brisk trot.

As he and Joe took the hobbles off the horses one by one, Delbert told him the names of each of them.

"Now, one of the most important things a wrangler has to do is to learn to know the horses, all of them and which cowboy they belong to. That'll take some time, but it's very important."

"I understand," Joe said. At least, he thought he understood. He certainly wanted to understand, wanted to know more about how and why these men, at least most of them, developed truly deep relationships with their horses.

"This here's Pokey," Delbert said, taking the hobbles off of a dapple grey mare.

Joe bent to take the hobbles off of a dark grey gelding. He struggled at first, but was able to get them off. "That's Smokey. He's one of Javier's scout horses," Delbert said.

Joe went to another horse. "What's his name?" he asked.

"That's Blue Rocket. He's a real speed demon, that one. Deacon rides him," Delbert replied.

And so they went. From horse to horse until at least a half an hour had passed, they went about taking the hobbles off, giving the horses freer range of motion. None of them wandered far however, as the day allowed them to see the others and stick together more easily. That was their natural tendency as herd animals.

The day wore on, with Delbert showing, teaching, coaching, quizzing, and reminding Joe about all manner of things a wrangler would need to know. The proper way to saddle a horse, quickly and efficiently. The proper way to create a makeshift picket line. What to watch for if the horses got nervous. How to use them as lookouts if danger was near. How to gather them when they scattered.

As the sun began to set, they saw a single rider approaching from the north.

"That'd be Javier," Delbert said. "Figured he'd be back from scouting about now."

The remuda was gathered a modest distance from Hucks' chuck wagon. Emmett was seated by the small coffee fire and saw him too. He quickly got to his feet. He made his way to his horse, still saddled and tied to the picket line with a few other mounts. He mounted and galloped out to meet Javier.

Delbert watched them as they walked their horses back to camp, and wondered what news Javier had about what lay ahead.

CHAPTER EIGHT

TEJANO

NEARLY TWO WEEKS HAD PASSED, with the drive making steady progress northward at a pace of ten or twelve miles a day. This would be considered quite normal for an average-sized herd, but with this Bar Nothin' herd numbered at well over five thousand, Emmett was quite pleased with the pace.

The drovers had begun to coalesce as a group, with some of the personality dynamics having either resolved themselves, or at least receded under the surface, so they were not an issue during the monotonous days and nights. Emmett hoped that would remain the case during the remainder of the drive. He hated to pay a man his wages and send him on his way, mid-stream. He wouldn't hesitate to do it, and the men knew it.

Emmett was also pleased with the progress Delbert had made with Joe. He really needed Delbert's full attention as his second in command, and Joe had made great strides in his education. He was quickly learning to effectively look after the remuda. Emmett was pleased with his effort and willingness to work hard, not only with the horses, but in helping Hucks with the chuck wagon.

It was near on dusk and most of the men were gathered around the coffee fire, eating their evening meal and talking with each other. Emmett made a note in his little notebook to speak with Hucks the next day about having Joe take over full time as wrangler of the remuda. He knew Hucks wouldn't be happy about losing his helper, despite his initial feelings when Joe arrived in camp. He had thought, quite mistakenly as it turned out, that Joe would be a burden. Some men seem to never be pleased, and are generally contrary by nature. This was, in general, a good description of Hucks.

Over the fire, Hucks' ubiquitous coffee pot was a fixture, and where it sat, the men knew to make their home for the evening. Several of the men were eating hungrily, quietly, too tired for conversation. Among them were Johnny and Deacon, who by this point had begun to, more or less, pay each other no notice, one no longer overtly wary of the other. Delbert was there too, as was Deacon, Javier, Ben, and Luke. The latter, in his boisterous voice, was the first to break the silence.

"Hucks, you sure you ain't part Meskin?" Luke said, his mouth still half full of beans.

"What's that supposed to mean?" Hucks replied.

"Nothin! Just that you cook like a Meskin, that's all."

"And what's a Mexican supposed to cook like, anyway?" Javier interjected.

Javier stared at Luke for a long moment, and in the absence of a response, set down his nearly empty plate and got to his feet. He picked up his saddle, which had been on the ground next to him, then walked out of the camp. His reaction belied something else on his mind, but he didn't say another word. He just walked off.

"What are you getting all bent out of shape about? You ain't a Meskin," Hucks called after Javier.

"Good! I mean it's good, for Lord's sake! Just sayin' I like the chuck. That's all!" Luke said to Hucks, but intending the response for Javier, truth be told.

Johnny leaned over to Delbert and added, "Sure got a way with words, don't he?"

"You ain't seen him full of whiskey yet," Delbert said.

"Yeah, he ain't funny like Hucks when he drinks. He just gets mean," Deacon added.

Johnny seemed displeased that Deacon has joined in the conversation as an equal. He said as much with his eyes as he glowered at Deacon.

"What?" Deacon asked.

"Nothin'," Johnny muttered, deciding that it was best to leave the situation be.

"Well not mean so much as mad," Delbert said to no one in particular. He turned his gaze to Johnny. "You got something to say, spit it out."

"What do you mean, Delbert? Mad about what?" Luke asked.

"Mad at the world. I don't know. Just mad," Delbert said.

"My Stepma used to get mad like that. Whiskey did it I reckon," Joe interjected. The men were surprised to hear Joe join in the conversation, and his small voice gave a lighter tone to it. "Then again, I 'spect I can't remember any time when she wasn't drinkin'," he continued.

"Moderation, boys. All things in moderation," Hucks

said in a jesting tone, overhearing and wanting to add his two cents. It was the closest thing the men had seen to Hucks being in a good mood thus far on the drive.

"All this whiskey talk and none to be had til Ft. Worth. Now there's something worth getting mad about," Luke said.

"Joe, you ought to go bed down the horses. You need any help?" Delbert said.

"No, sir. I can do it," Joe said.

"You sure, Joe?" Ben said, offering to help. Ben had been off to the side, pencil and notebook in hand.

"I'm sure. I wanna show Mr. Logan that I can paddle my own canoe," Joe said.

"Suit yourself," Ben said.

Hucks observed the exchange between Delbert, Ben and Joe. He would never admit it, not really even to himself, but the kid was starting to grow on him. He reflected back on what he'd lost so long ago, memories of a wife and two young sons burned to death in a fire he couldn't put out alone. Knowing his Beatrice was bedridden with a fever, unable to get out of bed herself, much less carry their infant son with her. His three year old son, Jack desperately trying to pull his mother out of bed as the burning rafters came down on them. If only he'd been plowing closer to the house. If only he'd seen the smoke sooner. If only…

He'd sought solace for many years in a whiskey bottle, and did so with entirely too much frequency still. He wanted to grab his bottle from its safe and secure hiding place in the back of his wagon, as he tried to forget his loss, as he tried to remember their faces and the peace of their home.

Joe got up and took his plate over to Hucks by the chuck wagon.

"Thank you Mr. Hucks, sir. I'm very grateful for the chow," Joe said.

His sudden appearance startled Hucks, jolting him back to the present and providing a helpful diversion from his desire for the bottle.

"Well don't go gettin' lazy and wantin' to sleep all the time like some of them boys do. Just cause your belly's full don't mean you can rest," Hucks said gruffly, the tone of his voice incongruent with the tender, at least by his standards, way he looked at Joe.

"Yes, sir," Joe said. He headed out of camp and into the young night to go tend to his horses.

The evening had grown darker and the light of the coffee fire had grown brighter by contrast.

"Hey Luke, you think maybe we could get up a card game? I've been learning some things and I think I might have a chance against you," Ben said as he poured himself some more coffee.

"Not likely. But if you wanna throw away some of your wages, it might as well be me who takes 'em," Luke replied.

Johnny scooted in a little closer to the fire and said, "Deal me in."

"Maybe I'll join you too, Luke, if Johnny Reb here'll allow a colored man in his game," Deacon said.

The night was made colder by the icy stare exchanged by Deacon and Johnny, neither men dropping his gaze.

"Aw, I'll take your money same as his," Luke said, jerking his head in the direction of Ben.

In the darkness, away from the camp, Javier tied up the front of his britches after having relieved himself. He picked his saddle back up and headed in the direction of the remuda, walking quietly and deliberately.

Not noticing Javier's approach, Joe was hobbling the horses, petting them and talking to them as he went. Javier smiled to himself as he heard Joe's voice, calm, sweet, and comfortable, as he spoke to the horses. It was good that Joe had taken Delbert's words to heart, as he did as well with the other men who took the time to work with him. He couldn't quite put his finger on it, but there was something he liked about Joe. Maybe it was the natural, gentle way he was able to get along with the horses. Maybe it was the alertness he saw, his eagerness to learn, to work, to be accepted as one worthy of the task he'd been assigned. Maybe it was his smile, seen most often when one of the horses responded well to one of his commands. Maybe it was the spirit, unbroken by his hard scrabble life, of the child who seemed willing to endeavor and to persevere no matter the challenge.

Javier reached the horses and deftly grabbed one, slipping the reins of his bridle over the horse's head. He took care to not let Joe see or hear him as he saddled the horse. Joe was oblivious to his presence until he spoke.

"Buenos noches, Jose."

"Evening, Javier. You headed out of camp?" Joe said, startled but not panicked. An important lesson that Delbert had imparted to him already was the importance of keeping calm around the horses at all times.

"Si. Going to scout. I'll be back by sun up," Javier said, looking around as he finished saddling the horse. "Stay sharp here. Holler for help if you hear or see anything strange, and listen to the horses. They'll sometimes tell you, by their actions, when there is danger near. Could be Commanches about, still. They'll come for the horses. A wrangler can never let anything happen to his remuda. I walked right into the herd here, and you didn't know I was here. You must do all you can to protect the remuda."

"Yes, sir. I'm sorry," Joe replied.

"You're still learning, Jose," Javier said as he mounted up.

"Javier, can I ask you something?"

Javier nodded.

"How come Hucks said you ain't a Meskin? That don't make no sense to me. Of course you're a Meskin."

Javier paused for a moment, considering the simplest way to explain. "My family did come from Mexico, Jose. But I am a Tejano." He paused another moment and leaned down, closer to Joe.

"Texas forever," he said, then turned his horse away from the remuda and headed off into the night.

Not quite understanding what Javier was getting at, Joe smiled and looked at him until he could no longer see him.

"Texas forever, Javier," he said, quietly enough so as not to startle the horses.

As Javier rode away, walking his horse slowly in the moonlit night, the voice of Papi, his father, came into his head. He recalled a conversation they had when he was very young, younger than Joe. He remembered it well as he carried its gravity with him each day, driving him to make a better life for his Rosa and the family they hoped to have.

They'd been digging a well all morning, delving deeper with great difficulty into the caliche which blocked their progress. His Papi always spoke of the caliche as a lesson of life.

"Javi, you have to dig past the caliche in life to get to the water. Water gives life in this country. If you can't get past the caliche, you die."

Javier took a short break from digging, hoping his Papi wouldn't scold him for it.

"Papi, why are we Tejano?" Javier asked, resting against the handle of his shovel.

"It's a long answer, Javi," Papi replied, leaning against his shovel as well.

"We have much time before we finish the well and our other chores. I want to know," Javier replied.

Pap sighed heavily, the weight of the words he wanted to say sitting heavy on his mind.

"I always say to you how important it is for you to have a son," he said. He looked into Javier's eyes. "Important to me."

"Si."

"It was important to my father before me," Papi said.

"But why?" Javier asked.

"My padre, your abuelo died in San Antonio, defending the Alamo against General Santa Anna's army. Both of my older brothers died there too."

"Si. Mama has told me," Javier said.

"I was a young boy, even younger than you. We were sent away from the mission before Santa Anna arrived," he said, his voice weakening. "The last words Father said to me before we were loaded in the wagon… His last words…" Papi said, his normally strong voice now trembling. "Never forget you are a Texan. Carry my blood with you for Texas."

"But are we not Mexican?" Javier asked.

"Our family came to Texas from Mexico, it's true. But we are no less Texan than the gringos who came from Tennessee or Alabama, or Germany, or England," he said as he drew his face closer to Joe. "Don't ever let anyone tell you that you are less."

Javier nodded his understanding and said, "I won't, Papi."

"Our people may have had Mexican blood, but our hearts will always be Texan," he said. "This is why you must carry the blood of Texas with you when you become a man."

"Texas forever," Javier said to his Papi, understanding the passion and importance of his father's words.

Javier's horse snorted loudly at some unseen distraction and he was brought back to the moment, the memory of his Papi receding into the rear reaches of his mind, as he scanned about the landscape, looking for some sign of what his horse may have noticed and been bothered by.

CHAPTER NINE

EASY TRAIL

THE NIGHT DRAGGED ON AND so did the card game. Emmett allowed the men to play as a diversion during what little down time they had between shifts. It was with the understanding that the stakes would be kept low and the men's spirits high. What he wouldn't abide was to have one of the men lose most or all of his wages to be paid at the end of the drive. That would be a sure fire recipe for poor morale, not only on the part of the sorry soul on the losing end of the gambling endeavor, but for the group of men as a whole. In order to be anything but disastrous, if not successful, a drive of this magnitude required that each man be ready, capable and motivated to do his job, and to have the respect of the other men. Much luck was needed as well. To have the seeds of disrespect sown amongst the men, or heaven forbid, for one of them to begin to bear the stench of ill fortune as a result of a game of poker would seriously dent the confidence of the men.

"Keep it light. Keep it easy," Emmett said whenever the topic of a card game was brought up.

"Darn it, kid! How can you be so lucky?" Johnny asked Ben, who had just laid down his hand of cards with a smile.

Delbert appeared to be asleep a bit away from the group gathered around the coffee fire, his hat over his eyes. Joe returned to camp. He found a seat from which to watch and quietly sat down. He was closest to Ben, but not so close as to interfere with the game.

"I'd accuse him of cheating but this is the only deck in camp, and I ain't let him deal yet," Luke said.

"I've been studying this game a bit, watching y'all play. Tried to learn a thing or two," Ben said.

"I say he's plain lucky. He plays long enough, that'll change," Johnny said impatiently.

"Ain't just luck. I heard tell of smart fellers that could work this game and win at it honest," Deacon added. "Young Ben here is smarter'n the three of us put together."

"Speak for yourself," Johnny said, his teeth ever so slightly gritted.

"I think that's enough for me tonight," Ben said.

He slowly got to his feet, but the other men protested vigorously.

"Got a feeling it's time for me to stop for the night. That's all," Ben said, his mind seemingly made up.

"You can't skin out before I get a chance to win my money back," Luke said, a tinge of anger in his voice. He looked at Johnny. "Say, lend me two dollars. I'm out if you don't."

"Nah, Luke. I may not be as smart as Ben here, but I know a bad bet when I see one."

Ben bent to pick up the pile of money he'd won which was still in the middle of the blanket spread on the ground.

He looked over at Joe and smiled with satisfaction. Joe returned the smile. He really liked Ben. He liked the way he conducted himself amongst the men, trying to learn the cowboy way, not just the work on the drive. He had settled into that with at least enough competency so as not to draw the ire of his uncle. More than that, Ben also seemed to show a genuine interest in who these men were, where they came from, and what was important to them. Joe liked that about Ben. He also liked that Ben, who was much younger than any of the other men with the exception of Joe himself. Ben never bossed him around or lorded over the fact that he was the nephew of the trail boss.

"Deacon, you're tighter'n a drum. I know you can spare it," Luke said.

Deacon shook his head slowly. He opened his mouth to speak, but didn't want to answer. "Luke, I..." he said.

"Luke, if I had any money, I'd go halfsies with you," Joe chimed in.

"That won't do me much good, now will it?" Luke snapped.

This appeared to give Ben an idea.

"Tell you what, Luke. I'll stake you that two dollars,"

"Well there's a good turn. Why that's downright Christian of you," Luke said.

"Fool," Deacon muttered, mostly to himself.

"I'll stake you for half. I'll put up the two dollars, but you give me half of what you win with it," he said.

Luke smiled at Ben's change of heart.

"One rule though," Ben said.

"Oh, you get to make the rules now, kid?"

"The one with the money always makes the rules, Luke. Everybody knows that," Johnny said.

"That's right," Deacon added, nodding in agreement.

"The rule is that you have to quit when I say. We'll split what's left when I call your game."

Luke paused for a moment. "Fair enough." He looked around and said, "Well? Deacon, deal us a hand."

Deacon shuffled the deck then dealt a hand to Luke, Johnny, and himself, with Ben looking on, his previous winnings safely tucked in the front pocket of his britches.

Delbert, who wasn't quite asleep, smiled from underneath his hat and let out a very quiet chuckle, as the game continued.

A few short hours later, the sky was ever so slightly brightening on the horizon to the east and the coffee fire had been reduced to smolders. Javier was still a good distance from the camp but was just able to make out the outline of the wagon and some of the horses. Most of the cattle were still bedded down, but an occasional faint lowing helped guide his way. He was on foot, leading his horse. Both he and the horse were limping noticeably.

It had been a long night for Javier. Despite some excellent farrier work he was able to do for the little paint mare, the deep stone bruise she had picked up somewhere in the night rendered her essentially incapable of bearing any weight. For his own part, Javier did not enjoy in the least walking in the dark for countless hours. Somewhere along the way he had twisted his ankle, an insult added to the injury dealt to him by having to walk afoot for so long. This was something he despised, which was, fortunately, quite foreign to him.

Javier had not been entirely truthful with Joe when he

said he was going to scout. While not really a lie, there was always something to learn and look for when he was out, he would hardly ever scout just overnight. Typically when he went out, he'd be gone for two or three days, sometimes longer. What Javier really wanted to do was to be away from camp, alone with his thoughts, alone with his memories of Rosa. So he did what he loved to do. He mounted up and rode. Out into the night he went, only to have his respite from camp spoiled by a lame horse and a sore, swollen ankle.

As he saw the outline of the camp, and the silhouettes of the horses and men ahead, he figured he'd have just about enough time to eat a fast breakfast, change mounts, and head back out. He didn't know for how long, but several days at least. He wouldn't return until he found the next place to water the herd. Something told him he should ride the Comanche bred mare.

The day had started like the others and became another of the ordinary sort. Breakfast at daybreak. The cattle coming alive as the graveyard shift came in to rest. A warm and humid morning slowly sliding into a hot and humid day. The herd creeping, slowly and steadily, northward. At times, progress felt as slow as molasses in the winter. They were moving the herd as fast as they could without causing significant weight loss, and therefore, economic value. On a good day, they might move ten or twelve miles. On days where there was good grazing for the herd, it might only be six or eight.

Deacon was on point, his usual spot. It was a challenging

place from which to work, and he spent more horses than the other men as a result. But Deacon was the man that Emmett trusted most of all when it came to keeping the herd moving in a true northward direction. Most of the time, it was a matter of directing the lead steer. Sometimes, a lead steer failed to reveal himself. Other times, more than one asserted himself for the role. More often than not, one stepped forward only to see his energy and fortitude wain, ceding his position to the next aspirant.

On this particular drive, Deacon counted himself most fortunate. The lead steer had lost his will to lead, falling back into the herd, which would have been very detrimental to the drive had it not been for another steer ready to take his place. By his reckoning, at least in physical terms, Deacon thought the beast was up to the job. His heart and courage were another matter entirely. Though they'd covered a good part of the journey already, there was still a very long way to travel, and most of it through some very rough and dry terrain in the Oklahoma territory. As Deacon admired the magnificent steer, his coloring a deep liver red with a wide strip of white down his chest and under his belly. The animal had horns as wide as Deacon was tall. He was beautiful stock and Deacon said a short, silent prayer for him. He prayed for his strength of body and of will. The prayer was by extension one for the drive as a whole, one for the safe conclusion to an arduous journey.

When the other men were out of earshot, he talked to the steer, calling him by the name he gave to every lead steer. He made the same promise to him that he'd made to the others, a secret promise of which only Deacon and Emmett were aware.

"You make it all the way to Abilene, Stepper, and I'll buy you at the yard. Mr. Logan and me will buy you and turn you out to graze your days away. That's right. Mr. Logan has kin near Abilene. They'll take you in and let you laze around with the horses 'til you join the Good Lord's herd."

He looked back to make sure none of the men could hear. "You just keep on steppin' and ol' Deacon will see to you when we make Abilene."

Deacon looked ahead and watched Joe moving the remuda along. He smiled as he thought about how the boy had taken to the trail and to his job as wrangler. A little ahead of Joe and the remuda, Hucks could be seen with the chuck wagon. Emmett was traveling alongside the wagon, lost in his thoughts, worrying about all manner of things as one would expect of the Trail Boss.

Hucks would be breaking for the mid-day meal soon and Joe needed to move the remuda ahead of the wagon so he'd have time to build the rope corral and gather the horses. This was necessary so the men could change mounts after they ate.

"Joe, go ahead and set up just past that little stand of Mesquites up yonder on that bluff. Shouldn't take more'n an hour for me to get there," Hucks called out to Joe as he drove the remuda past the wagon.

Joe was dressed in the same pitiful coveralls he was wearing when he came into their camp. He was wearing a shirt that Delbert had given him that was many sizes too big for him, with the sleeves rolled up high enough to keep them out of the way.

"Yes, sir," Joe called back to him. Hucks didn't acknowledge his response, so Joe wasn't sure he'd heard it.

The exchange appeared to catch the interest of Emmett, who departed his own thoughts and watched Joe and the remuda pull away from the wagon, putting more and more distance between them.

"That boy might be a keeper after all," Emmett said. "I didn't think there was much to him at first, but..." Emmett looked over at Hucks who now appeared lost in thoughts of his own. "You alright over there Hucks?"

Hearing Emmett speak his name, Hucks returned to the moment.

"Damn pitiful sight."

"What?" Emmett asked.

"That boy," Hucks said, with a deep sadness in his voice. Emmett didn't know what to say, but he knew what Hucks meant.

They went along in silence for a few minutes, then the silence was shattered by a loud whoop from one of the boys back with the herd. It was Luke.

Luke took off running on his horse, running at a full gallop and giving chase to something no one else seems to be able to see. He swung his loop furiously, and yelled back over his shoulder.

"A dollar says I can get a loop on him in one try."

Clear from the dust, several of the men could suddenly see Luke is giving chase to a jack rabbit, trying to rope the varmint.

Delbert called after him. "I'll take that!"

"Me too!" Deacon added.

Ben rode up next to Delbert.

"You think he can do it?" he asked.

"Good chance. Luke is as handy with a loop as any cowboy ever went up the Chisholm Trail," Delbert replied.

Luke swung a large loop that was true to its mark but the speedy jackrabbit slipped through it before Luke could pull his slack and close the loop.

"Ah hell, I had him!" Luke said in frustration. He paused for a second then, organizing a new, smaller loop, called to Deacon and Delbert.

"Double or nothing!"

"Done," said Deacon.

"Done," agreed Delbert.

"Ha! Let me show you how it's done," Luke said, as he kicked his horse back into motion.

He flushed the jackrabbit out from under the bush he'd found to hide behind, and once again the chase was on. Luke swung his rope several times rapidly above his head, steering his horse with his left hand as he measured his chances. He then threw a long loop from further away than he would have liked, but he feared he was losing the little speed demon. The loop closed on the rabbit's midsection. Luke stopped his horse quickly and started pulling the rabbit closer so it couldn't escape.

"Ha ha! There you have it boys!" Luke said, laughing out loud, as the men did the same, yelling their congratulations over the din of the cattle lowing.

"Well dang if he didn't actually do it," Delbert said.

"Pay up, boys!" Luke said.

Hucks had stopped his wagon, figuring that where they were was a good enough spot to pitch his tent and make the mid-day meal. He and Emmett had observed the proceedings and they were now within earshot of Luke.

"Hey Hucks! No sowbelly for me tonight! I caught him, I eat him!" Luke shouted to him, still laughing.

Emmett, though somewhat annoyed at Luke's foolish waste of his horse's capacity, couldn't help but crack a smile.

"You skin him, I'll cook him," Hucks hollered back.

"Done," Luke said.

Javier had approached from the northwest and drawn close to Emmett and Huck's wagon. Delbert had noticed Javier's approach and ridden up to the wagon as well.

"Buenos días, Emmett," Javier said, then acknowledged the others. "Delbert. Hucks."

"Any news?" Emmett asked.

"Good water by day's end," Javier responded.

"That's good to hear. Should make Ft. Worth in two, maybe three days," Emmett said.

"I saw Commanche sign, but it looked stale. Maybe a week or more."

Emmett nodded his understanding. He said to Delbert, "Put three men on the night watch for the remuda, just in case. I'll be damned if I'm gonna lose my horses to a bunch of Commanches when we're pushing five thousand head of cattle."

"Will do. Consider it done," Delbert replied.

"Delbert, would you send Joe to rustle me up some wood. I'm pretty sure I won't have enough for the mid-day meal," Hucks said, not noticing Joe approaching on his horse dragging a pile of wood tied up in some canvas behind him. While the others had been enjoying the distraction of Luke's antics, Joe had built his rope corral, gathered and grained the remuda inside it, and somehow found the time to gather some wood for Hucks' fire.

"I think he's a step ahead of us," Delbert said with a big grin.

The sun was high in the sky, which held only a small cloud or two. There was no sign of foul weather. It was a fine day. Hucks thought that it was hotter than it should be for late spring. The ground seemed drier than he remembered in past years. The men were having their mid-day meal. Some of them were sitting near the small coffee fire, but most of them were sharing a modicum of shade provided by the makeshift canvas lean-to they'd built. It was hot in the sun, and there was no breeze to speak of. The little bit of shade the canvas cover offered gave some respite from the direct sun, which caused them to linger a bit over their food. They were willing to risk a sharp rebuke from Emmett.

Hucks was sitting by his wagon, desperately trying to thread a needle. He always brought along some needles and thread, as well as a bolt of cloth, in case he needed to patch one of the men's clothes, or in a pinch, even the wagon cover.

He held the needle up close and made another futile attempt to slip the thread through its eye. Frustrated, he held the needle away from him, nearly at arm's length then tried again, to no avail. He tried once more, trying again to hold the needle close to him.

"Damn eyes. Not worth spit no more," he said to himself, his anger manifesting in a quick motion of his hands towards his lap. This earned him a sharp prick from the needle.

"Owww!" he cried out, surprising himself with how loud he said it and catching the attention of Ben, who was sitting in the shade.

"Hey Ben! Come over here," Hucks said.

Ben complied, approaching with a bit of trepidation. He'd learned already to be wary of Hucks when he was in one of his moods.

"You out of wood already, Hucks? I thought you'd have enough for at least the evening meal," Ben said.

"Nah. I got plenty," Hucks said.

He handed Ben the needle and thread. "You've got young eyes. See if you can thread this here needle for me."

"Sure thing," Ben said, a bit perplexed.

It took Ben a couple of tries, but he finally got it, and handed the needle and thread back to Hucks.

"Can't say I've had a lot of practice," Ben said.

"Well what makes you think I have?" Hucks said in a testy tone.

Ben's brow furrowed, not sure what to make of Hucks' mood or why he was so intent on threading a needle in the middle of the day.

"Well then…" he said. "I guess I'd better get saddled up and go relieve the other boys so they can eat."

"Well go ahead then," Hucks said in the same testy tone.

It was the bewildered look on Ben's face that caused to Hucks to realize how angry he sounded. *Listen to yourself,* he thought to himself.

"Thank ya, son," He said to Ben, in a much softer tone.

"Anytime," Ben said, shaking his head as he walked away to grab his saddle and return to work.

Hucks commenced to sew a passable seam on the pieces of cloth he'd cut from the bolt he brought along in the wagon. His hands were a bit shaky, which caused him to mess up the last few stitches in the seam.

"Dammit!" he said as he undid the poor stitches so he could do them over. Unseen by Hucks, some of the other men had come over to see what he was doing.

"Hucks, what the devil are you up to?" Delbert asked.

"You thinking of leavin' the drive and takin' up a job as a seamstress when we get to Ft. Worth?" Luke also asked.

"Ain't you boys got some cattle to move? Y'all get on out of here and leave ol' Hucks alone, or I'll piss in your coffee tonight," Hucks said.

"You mean you ain't been doin' that all along?" Deacon said.

They all burst out in laughter, with the exception of Johnny, who just stared at Deacon.

It had been nearly two weeks since Lucy had met Ben at the picnic after church. She couldn't stop thinking about him. Thinking of how handsome he was in his traveling suit, which he'd worn when they first met. Thinking of how rugged he looked in the trail clothes he'd changed into when he came back on his horse. Thinking of how he stood up to her father with a strength of resolve she'd not seen in anyone she'd ever met before. She imagined spending time with him, how he could make her feel happy and free. She imagined he was as kind to everyone as he'd been to her. She imagined how she could spend her life with him, have a family with him.

Lucy knew that she was running out of time to get a letter posted for Ben to receive when he passed through Fort Worth. She was impatient and fidgety through-out dinner that night, eating just a few bites before asking to be excused. All she wanted to do was be alone in her room, alone with her thoughts of Ben, alone with the letter she'd written to Ben soon after they met. She was sorely afraid she wouldn't get it out on time, afraid that it would miss Ben. She was mostly afraid that she would never see him again.

As she ascended the stairs up to her room, she vowed that no matter the obstacles imposed by her mother, who normally met her in the afternoons to stroll home together after Lucy's school day was done, she would find a way to post the letter. Somehow, some way, she would get the letter to Ben, even if her father, whose offices were situated directly across the street, saw her enter or leave the post office. He would know why she went there, and she didn't care. She couldn't risk not seeing Ben ever again. She just simply couldn't.

Lucy entered her bedroom and set the coal oil lamp down on the side of the dressing table. It was dusk and the light was dim. She sat down in the small chair at the dressing table and began to let her hair down. Slowly the auburn locks fell down on her shoulders. She brushed it for a long while, thinking how it would feel if it were Ben's hand stroking her hair. She looked at her face in the mirror as she put down the brush, and then gently put her hand to her cheek. A smile slowly came to her face.

She quietly got up from her dressing table and walked to the door of her room, putting her ear to it to listen for approaching footsteps. Hearing none, she quickly and quietly pulled an envelope from within the pages of the bible on the little table beside her bed. She went back to her dressing table and turned up the lamp to make the room bright enough to read the letter.

She grew quietly giddy as she read the letter to herself, once again, perhaps for the hundredth time.

Dear Ben,

I hope this letter finds you well and happy in your new situation. In fact, I will be happy if it finds you at all.

I have had quite a hard time concentrating on my studies in the days since we met. I can't seem to stop thinking about our brief time together and what it meant to me.

No one has ever stood up to my father before. You can be most assured that he hates you for it, and yet, I believe he respects you for it as well.

Did you really mean that you would come back for me? I do truly want it to be so. However scandalous it may be for me to agree to court without my father's permission, if you feel as you claimed, then I will gladly bear the price of that scandal.

If it sustains you on your long and dangerous journey, please know that each day that passes is a day the rapid completion of which I long for, so that the next will bring me that much closer to the time we can see each other again.

May the Lord Bless and keep you until then.

Your faithful admirer,
Lucy

Lucy clutched the letter to her chest, then looked at her face in the mirror. She had a passing thought about how silly it was that she was so smitten by a young and handsome stranger who'd only just passed through town, briefly and out of her life. That passing thought was easily dismissed with the beautiful thought of Ben holding her hand, then the thought of Ben holding *her*. She blushed in spite of herself, and smiled again at her face in the mirror. She carefully refolded the letter and slid it back into its envelope, determined that tomorrow, no matter the risk of discovery, she would post the letter.

Later, when she lay in bed, vainly trying to fall asleep, she said a prayer that the letter would find Ben, and that he was the man of his word that she believed him to be.

CHAPTER TEN

TOWN

I T WAS SATURDAY IN THE early afternoon. The herd had arrived slightly to the south and west of Fort Worth, their progress slowed a bit by weather. The Trinity River was swollen from two days of rain that had fallen as the drive had worked its way northward, and they'd have to cross both the West Fork of the river, and then the Clear Fork. Emmett had originally planned to take the drive east of Dallas, and thus only have to cross the river once, south of the city. However, Javier had convinced him that the prior two or three drives that had gone before them had taken that route, and that there would be much better grass for grazing if they took the route west of Fort Worth. This would allow the herd to maintain, if not gain some weight, prior to heading into the much drier country north of the Red River in the Oklahoma territory.

Even though the rain had slowed them down by a day or so, and additionally they would have to hold the herd south of Fort Worth for a couple of more days while the river receded, Emmett was pleased with the pace they had been able to maintain. The herd was in good shape and the men were working pretty well together. Given the time, the drive would be held up before they could cross the Trinity, it made sense to let most of the men go into town to kick up their heels before they got back underway. The cattle had plenty to graze on and so would be content for a day or so.

Emmett gave them until dusk on Sunday to be back in camp, figuring a little over a day wouldn't give too much opportunity to get in any trouble that couldn't be easily dealt with. He kept Joe back to look after the remuda, and Deacon along with two of the other boys to look after the cattle. Those men would be needed to keep them bunched if they started to wander. He let the rest of the men go, in staggered departures, a few at a time. Emmett stayed in camp with Hucks, not wanting to chance any kind of dust up in town, which could endanger the drive. Fort Worth, like all cowtowns, was a very unpredictable place, and it wasn't hard at all to find oneself in a sticky situation. These often led a man to fight or shoot his way out.

The last time he'd gone into Fort Worth was nearly ten years before, and Emmett decided, even back then, that it was too wild and wooly for a man who wanted to focus on business.

Before Delbert left for town with Luke, Johnny and Ben, Emmett had handed him a letter to be posted. Ordinarily, Emmett wouldn't send Mr. Callaway a report on the state of the drive so early in the journey, but given the size of the herd, he thought it prudent. He had the opportunity to get a letter posted.

Luke, Ben, Johnny and Delbert were riding four abreast as they traveled away from the herd and in the direction of

Fort Worth and its infamous red light district, the first to be known as Hell's Half Acre.

"How long do you think it will take us to get there, Delbert?" Ben asked.

"At least an hour, maybe two, I think. Hopefully no longer than that. I have to stop at the post office first to send a letter to Mr. Callaway for Emmett, so we'd better get there before it closes, else he'll skin me," Delbert replied.

"Oh, let me do it for you. I was planning on going there anyway. I am hoping there'll be a letter waiting for me there. Not likely, to be sure, but hoping for it," Ben said.

"Nice of you to offer, but I think I should take it there myself. You're welcome to come along with me, if you want," Delbert replied.

Ben blushed, which Delbert found to be quite curious.

"Expecting a letter from your mother?"

Ben shrugged sheepishly and said, "Not exactly."

"Want me to pick it up for you?" Delbert said with a grin.

"Oh, heavens no! I couldn't let you do that! Like I said, it's not likely to be there anyway." Ben said.

"It's just as well you start out in town with me. Lord only knows what these boys will get you into this evening."

"I'm excited to see it. Well, the Hell's Half Acre part. I've seen a good bit of the rest of Fort Worth," Ben said.

"You just stay close to me, kid. It's a mighty wild place, and a helluva place to get into trouble," Luke said to Ben.

"Somethin' you'd know a lot about, Luke," Delbert said.

"It's true I've raised my share of hell, but I was always just havin' some fun. This is the last trip to town 'til we make Abilene at the end of the drive. That's a mighty long time without whiskey and women."

"And I'm sure you'll be leaving Ft. Worth with half your wages lost to whiskey and women," Johnny said.

"Yeah, but a dollar says I'll have more fun than all you boys put together," Luke said.

"Fun? You can't be serious. Knowin' how you handle your whiskey?" Delbert said. "Say, Johnny. I got a dollar says Luke spends at least one night in Marshall Crawford's jailhouse."

Johnny said, "No way I'd take that bet."

"It's so exciting. I can't wait to try my luck at a real table," Ben said.

Ben looked to one side, then the other, noticing something peculiar, something he hadn't noticed before

"Hey, I'm the only one here without a gun," he said.

Delbert was sporting a Colt Single Action 45 pistol, the one they called the Peacemaker. Luke was carrying the same pistol, but an older model, made before the war. Johnny had a Cooper Double Action revolver, an older model, but one that meant even more serious business than the Peacemaker. The double action meant it could be fired simply by pulling the trigger rather than having to cock the hammer first. It was a gunfighter's gun. Delbert had taken note of it as they were leaving camp.

"Watch yourself and don't do anything stupid or sudden. Just stay close to us, and you won't need one," Delbert said, the gravity in his voice registering quite clearly. "Lot of trouble in Hell's Half Acre, and you don't have to look for it. It'll find you."

Johnny had a particularly dour look on his face in response to Delbert's advice.

"Johnny, ain't you lookin' forward to a night in town?" Luke asked.

"Sure I'm looking forward to town. 'Specially finding me a soiled dove to ease my troubles. It's a far piece to Abilene," Johnny replied.

"Well you'd all best ride a wide circle around a gal named Helga if you catch sight of her. Last time we were through she was working over at the Bella Donna," Delbert said. Then he looked squarely at Ben. "Especially you."

Luke grinned at the look of surprise that came over Ben's face.

"I suggest a bath, a shave and a haircut before you hit a saloon. If you don't do it first, you won't do it," Delbert added.

"Ben, you can skip the shave," Johnny said. He laughed a little and the others smiled too.

"Nice to see you ain't always such a sour puss," Delbert said.

The faintest of piano sounds, punctuated by the occasional loud outburst from distant voices, came within earshot. It grew louder, and Ben's excitement grew more difficult to contain, as they drew closer to town. He didn't know what to expect in Hell's Half Acre, and he dared not have any expectation of what might await him at the post office.

Still he hoped for the best, on both counts.

The evening was well underway in Hell's Half Acre. Most of the saloons were fairly crowded with patrons. Delbert and the boys, all freshly bathed and shaven, walked along the thoroughfare and approached the Dove. It was one of the more notorious establishments in the district, with a tough reputation, not only with respect to its typical patrons, but also the sort of women who worked the upstairs. They were the joint's namesake to hear tell of it, soiled doves most of whom were beyond redemption by all but the church. Patrons of the Dove were mostly trail hands, mule skinners, railroad workers and two-bit gamblers. Not the most desirable clientele to say the least.

Ben thought the place sounded outraged as they drew close. Angry, drunken voices emanated from inside. Even the piano music had an ireful beat. The sound of crashing glass penetrated the din of the street as two men tumbled out of the window, clothes and skin torn by the shards of the broken pane. Delbert, Johnny, Luke and Ben all stopped in their tracks.

"Watch yourself, boys. Stay still. Scatter if you see one pull a pistol," Delbert said.

The two men rolled out into the street as they tussled. One was shorter than the other, but stockier and a bit older. The other was lean and quick. They punched and kicked and clawed each other as a crowd gathered to watch the melee. There didn't seem to be a clear favorite of the crowd. The onlookers simply cheered for whichever appeared to have the upper hand at a given moment. The tall man would gain the advantage for a few seconds, only to lose it to the shorter man. Then, he'd regain it again. Punching, kicking, growling. On it went for what seemed to Ben quite a while, though in reality it probably wasn't more than a minute or two. The two men exhausted themselves as the crowd let them fight it out, with neither man clearly besting the other. They separated and lay next to each other in the street, chests heaving.

"Let's go, fellers. Nothing much else to see here. The Marshall won't come without gun fire. The Bella Donna is just a little further up the street, and it should be a good bit tamer than this slaughterhouse," Delbert said to the others.

The Bella Donna was a busy saloon. Its patrons, consisting of quite a few cowboys and a number of nicely dressed men from town, seemed to be enjoying themselves. A piano player was entertaining the men as the few women working the room circulated, making small talk here and there, and actively inviting the men to go upstairs to have a more private encounter. Most of the men were seated at tables of four or more around the room, playing faro or poker. A few were at the bar, drinking whiskey. Some were sullen, some were not, and they were all there for reasons not openly shared with others.

Delbert walked into the Bella Donna and eyed the room slowly. Johnny did the same. Luke, with whiskey and more on his mind, barreled past them and headed straight for the bar. "Outta my way, boys. There's a bottle over there with my name on it."

Ben stood behind Delbert, eagerly trying to get a glance at the sites inside that went with the sounds he'd heard as they approached.

Luke reached the bar and impatiently summoned the bartender. "Barkeep! A bottle and a glass."

The bartender replied, "You got money?" as he cast a side glance at Luke.

"Of course I've got money. What do I look like?"

"A broke saddle tramp making his last stop before

heading north to Kansas, a broke man who won't get paid until he gets there. That's where I'd put my money," he replied condescendingly.

Luke reached in his pocket, fishing for an uncomfortably long time before finding the quarter he was looking for. Then, he slammed the coin down on the bar, glaring at him. The bartender placed a bottle of whiskey and the shot glass in front of Luke, then picked up and inspected the quarter. Luke uncorked the bottle and poured a shot, drank it in one swallow and quickly poured another.

Delbert, Johnny, and Ben joined Luke at the bar, but none sat down.

Delbert said to the bartender, "A bottle and a couple of glasses, if you please."

He turned to Ben and asked, "Have you ever drank whiskey before?"

"No I haven't." Ben replied, shaking his head.

Delbert turned to the bartender and said, "Make that three glasses." Johnny grinned, but Luke was oblivious, as he poured himself another shot.

The bartender brought the bottle and three shot glasses. Delbert uncorked in the bottle and field each of the glasses, handing one to Johnny, and another to Ben.

"Well boys, welcome to Hell's Half Acre," Delbert said. "Ben, I'm going to counsel you to take it easy with this stuff. Even two or three shots will make your mind mighty foggy."

A few minutes passed. Luke was enthusiastically tossing back whiskey, matching Delbert and Johnny three for one. Ben was taking it all in, enjoying the scene of his first trip to a real saloon. He was slowly sipping his whiskey, and attempting to do so with a straight face.

Delbert surveyed the room.

"There she is boys. Ain't she a sight?" he said.

Helga was making small talk with some patrons at a table across the room. The men seemed to enjoy her presence, even as they attempted to continue their card game. She was a very robust and rotund woman, taller and larger than many of the men in the room. She wore a long dress that went nearly to the floor. Her corset was cinched tight, and it was clear that quite a battle must have ensued earlier between it and the unlucky soul charged with helping her get dressed. There was a lot of woman underneath that corset. Her dark brown hair was pinned up and she smelled of too much perfume. It was a present from a frequent customer in town. She didn't really care for the customer, but she liked the money he spent, and she liked the smell of the perfume, so she was not shy in its application.

Ben saw her as well and his eyes widened in fear. Delbert saw Ben's reaction.

"She'll take care of three or four boys like you before breakfast," Delbert said.

Johnny played along with Delbert's teasing. Luke kept tossing back whiskey, not seeming to notice.

"I hear tell she likes 'em real young and innocent, too," Johnny said.

"Like you, Ben," Delbert said, nudging him with his elbow, barely able to contain his laughter.

Helga looked up from her conversation and saw Ben

staring at her. She was intrigued by the four men standing at the bar, the young one in particular.

Well, hello there! she thought to herself as she got up and made her way in their direction, her eyes squarely focused on Ben. She'd seen a lot of young men pass through the Bella Donna, but this one was particularly enticing. He was quite handsome, though not uniquely so. He had an air about him, one that said he didn't quite fit in with the men he was with. That quality was very attractive to her, though she wouldn't be able pinpoint precisely why if she were asked.

Delbert and Johnny laugh. "She's on the hunt and she sees her prey," Delbert said.

Ben was apoplectic, feeling trapped as he cast his eyes wildly about the room. The low cut of her dress, which barely covered the top of the corset, made it exceedingly difficult for Ben to ignore what he thought might be the biggest bosoms he'd ever seen. He tugged hard on Luke's sleeve.

"Luke! Come on! A couple of chairs just opened up over there. Let's jump in the game," he said, desperate to avoid a conversation with the oncoming huntress.

Without looking back at the others, Ben headed to the poker table with two open seats. Luke reluctantly followed, bottle in hand, leaving the shot glass on the bar.

Helga got distracted with another table of patrons, one of whom she knew well, who pawed at her. Ben appeared exceedingly relieved and his sigh confirmed it, as he and Luke sat down at the table. They acknowledged their neighbors, exchanging introductory pleasantries, though Luke's were quite perfunctory. Ben and Luke anted up as their hands were dealt by a small and very round man with very close-set squinty eyes.

"Jacks or better to open," he said to Luke and Ben as he deftly dealt the cards to them and the other two men at the table.

Delbert and Johnny remained at the bar, watching proceedings around the room.

"I always liked this place. My favorite place in Cowtown," Delbert said.

"I've only been through Ft. Worth once, right after the war. Before this place opened," Johnny replied.

"Comanche hunter?" Delbert asked.

Johnny nodded. "Had to have somethin' to do. We all did."

"That's true, I reckon," Delbert replied.

Johnny tossed back a shot of whiskey and caught the eye of one of the ladies working the room — a short, fiery headed lass who was somewhat less rotund than most of the other women working the saloon. She had a young, pretty face with a few freckles. It was marred only by a noticeable scar across her cheek, which ran from near her ear almost to her nose, a lifelong reminder of the perils of her profession. The young woman appeared quite bored with the men sitting at the table where she was currently situated. Holding Johnny's gaze, the woman got up from the table and headed to the stairs leading to the upstairs rooms. She motioned for Johnny to follow her.

Johnny drew a deep breath. It wasn't a nervous breath, but one borne more of resignation.

"I'll be a little while upstairs," he said.

"Take your time," Delbert replied dryly. "I'll be here."

He poured himself another drink, took a sip and resumed gazing around the room, in large part looking for potential trouble. Trouble could erupt quickly in a place where whiskey, guns, and men without much to lose, were all thrown together.

Johnny followed the woman up the stairs, exchanging no words.

Across the room, Luke and Ben were having mixed success at the table.

"I call," Luke seethed.

The man seated next to Luke laid down his cards, grinned, and raked the pot towards his existing pile of money. He was called Blister by his friends, a small man but a sharp one, who by his appearance was no stranger to the tables in establishments such as the Bella Donna.

"Dammit. I'm out," Luke said bitterly as he pulled a draw from his whiskey bottle and considered his now fully depleted resources. He looked over at Ben, his gaze by no means friendly.

"Stake me for half?" Luke asked, though it didn't really sound like a question.

Ben, feeling quite intimidated to say the least, looked across the room at Delbert, vainly hoping for some guidance, but Delbert's gaze was elsewhere.

"All right, but same rule as before. We quit when I say," Ben replied, mustering as much confidence and authority as he could.

"Have it your way, then," Luke said, his voice tinged with anger. He took another swig from the whiskey bottle, now much closer to empty than before.

Blister and the other player at the table, a tall, lanky

acquaintance of his looked at each other and grinned. They were happy to have found a patsy who was well on his way to being drunk and who had a kid at the table to bankroll him. It was going to be a good night – for them.

A couple of hours passed.

Johnny, who had returned from upstairs in a much more relaxed frame of mind, rejoined Delbert at the bar. They both were watching events unfold at the table where their compatriots continued playing cards.

Ben and Luke were, surprisingly, holding their own at the poker table with Blister and the tall man. Luke's luck had turned somewhat, and combined with Ben's clear head and quick mind, they had been able to win back a goodly portion of what Luke had lost earlier in the evening. Given their improved situation, which Luke took to be a direct result of his skill, he did not take kindly at all when they lost the next hand.

Luke went to take another drink of whiskey but his bottle was empty, same as it was the prior two times he attempted to take a drink.

"Bring us another bottle!" Luke yelled angrily in the direction of the bartender.

Ben placed his hand on Luke's arm.

"Luke, it's time to go. We can count when we get back to camp."

"Get your damn hands off me, boy!"

Ben recoiled, afraid, for the first time, really afraid of Luke.

"Take it easy! A deal's a deal, now it's time to go."

"Well I ain't through playin'. If you wanna skin out, then go ahead," Luke said.

Luke took the pile of money in front of him and crudely peeled off what looked to be half of it.

"There. There's your half. Now git," he said, motioning Ben away with his hand. "I don't need no snot-nosed greenhorn kid ruinin' my good time anyhow."

He turned his head in the direction of the bar. "Where's my bottle, dammit?"

Across the room, still standing at the bar, Delbert and Johnny continue to watch.

"You think we ought to step in?" Johnny asked Delbert.

"Nah. I have a hunch Ben can handle it. Pour us a drink."

Johnny obliged, pouring them each a shot into their glasses.

Back at the poker table, Ben was putting his pile of money away in a saddle bag, including the money Luke had shoved his direction.

The patrons at the surrounding tables, and indeed in the whole saloon had begun to take notice of the rising noise and tension emanating from Ben and Luke's table.

"Luke, I know you're drunk and your head's not clear, but you need to listen to me. I'm telling you, it's time for us to go," Ben said.

"Nobody tells me when to leave or when to stay!" Luke said.

Luke uneasily got up out of his chair and attempted to shove Ben away. In the process, he fell over the table and crumpled to the ground.

"Go ahead, son. This won't end well. Take your winnin's and head on out," Blister said to Ben.

"That's right. Get on out of here," Luke said, as he clumsily tried to get back to his feet.

Ben cast a glance in the direction of Delbert and Johnny.

He mouthed the words, "What do I do?"

Delbert didn't respond other than to just toss his head in the direction of the door.

"Why don't you ride back with him. I'll stay and wait to get Luke out of here and back to camp when he's sobered up a bit. Ain't no use tryin' now," Delbert said to Johnny. "He's like a comin' storm. Sometimes all you can do is wait for it to blow over. We'll be along directly, probably after daybreak."

"All right. I'll let Emmett know," Johnny replied. He motioned toward Luke. "Good luck there."

"Not the first time," Delbert said.

Delbert turned his back to the room and faced the bar, slowly taking a sip from his glass.

Johnny finished his glass, quickly poured another, and just as quickly threw that one back, then headed for the door. Ben got to the door at about the same time, glancing back over his shoulder at Luke as he walked out.

Luke sat back down at the table in a huff, trying the best he could, in his condition, to appear that we wasn't actually in that condition.

"All right then. Now that we got rid of the young'un, us men can get down to business."

None of the men at the table responded.

Luke looked at his empty bottle, getting angrier.

"Barkeep!" he yelled over his shoulder. "Dammit! Where's my bottle?"

Luke picked up his empty bottle from the table and

threw it across the room, narrowly missing another table of patrons and the piano player.

The bottle crashed against the wall and the room grew silent. Nearly every man in the room had drawn his gun. Luke went for his as well, but it was gone.

"Dammit! Where's my pistol? Somebody took my pistol!"

Outside the Bella Donna, Johnny and Ben wordlessly mounted up and headed out of town. As they faded into the night, toward the herd, Ben reassured himself that the letter from Lucy was still safely tucked in his pocket, then gently fingered the pistol shoved in his belt.

CHAPTER ELEVEN

GHOSTS

JOE SAT CLOSE TO THE remuda. He'd found a flat piece of rock that would serve as his watch area, and eventually a place for him to bunk for the night. It was set up higher than the surrounding ground and about the size of the back of Hucks' chuck wagon. Joe hoped it would serve as a bit of snake deterrent, though the horses usually served him well in that regard.

The night was extremely dark, with only the slightest moonlight silhouetting the horses. The air was still and heavy, stifling and muggy. Joe was uncharacteristically nervous. He soothed himself by rolling up his shirt sleeves, rolling them down, then repeating the process over and over, a nervous, subconscious tic, which had earned him a violent rebuke from his stepmother on more than one occasion. Yet still he continued, not realizing, rolling one sleeve up above his elbow, smoothing its folds, unfolding it back down to his wrist, before moving on to the other sleeve. He had to remind himself to breathe as he tried to dispatch the sense of dread, which was as heavy as the air.

Normally, he was very comfortable around the horses, a

fact that both Delbert and Emmett had picked up on right away when he came into their camp. He'd taken to them quickly and easily, and they to him, as he quickly got to know them all, their names and their personalities.

But tonight, he was nervous, this being the darkest night he'd had to contend with as wrangler. There was only a small handful of men to tend the herd. The horses were nervous too. Joe hoped it was he who was making them uneasy, and not the horses being uneasy about some unseen menace.

The horses nickered and milled about. Every sound the horses made and every sound the night made seemed to make Joe jump. That included the low sound of footsteps he heard, not hurried steps, and only one set as best he could tell, but he shivered just the same.

"Joe? You all right out here?" came a voice from the same direction as the footsteps. Joe jumped at first, then sighed in relief as he realized who it was.

"Figured you could use some company," Deacon said as his dark silhouette came into Joe's view.

"Howdy, Deacon. Shouldn't you be out on the graveyard shift?" Joe asked. "Say, how'd you see where I was sittin' here in the dark?"

"Aww, ol' Deacon sees real good, near and far, day and night. Somethin' not a whole lotta folks know about me," he replied, as he sat down on the rock next to Joe.

"I asked Emmett if I could help you watch the remuda," he said, the white of his smile showing in dark.

"I'm all right. It's just kinda dark tonight," Joe said.

"You scared?"

"I dunno. I reckon maybe a little."

"What's scarin' ya?"

"Oh, I don't know. I know I oughtn't be. But I kinda get skeered of things I can't see."

"Comanches?"

Joe nodded nervously, though he wasn't sure Deacon could see him.

"Well they ain't near as bad as when I first came to Texas, but that don't mean a band won't make a run at the horses."

"I hear they treat horses like gold," Joe said.

"Well horses is like money to them, if that's what you mean."

"I heard they... I heard they take *folks* too," Joe said, his voice betraying the fear he felt.

"There's some truth to that, I gotta say. Mostly just the young girls. They need 'em to have their babies so as to help keep the tribe alive. Their squaws ride horses good as their braves and they lose a lot of babies 'cause of it."

Deacon paused, not sure if he should continue.

"Men they usually just kill soon's they can," he said, deciding that Joe was man enough to hear the truth. It pained him to see Joe shudder as the words left his mouth.

"Ain't near as many as they used to be. Cholera done killed most of 'em off," Deacon continued. "Army's just about starved out the rest."

"Still pretty scary to think about 'em comin' for us though," Joe said.

"I 'spect we won't have any trouble, but just as well for us to keep our eyes sharp. Ears too," Deacon said. "If any come around, they'll mostly want the horses, maybe a beef or two. You ever shoot a gun?"

"Just an old rifle of my pa's for huntin' squirrels and rabbits and the like."

"Well after you've grow'd up a little more, maybe I can talk Delbert into letting me teach you to shoot a pistol. If you keep ridin' with us, you'll need to be able to shoot horseback."

"That'd be real fine," Joe said.

He paused to reflect for a moment. "Deacon?"

"Yeah?"

"It sure seems you and Johnny don't take much of a shine to each other," Joe said.

Deacon paused to consider his answer. There's so much he would have liked to say to Joe, so much to get off his chest, so much that needed to be said.

"We're just different kinds of folks. That's all," Deacon said.

"Seems to me that folks is folks, ain't they?" Joe replied. "Especially out here."

"Not everybody sees it that way, Joe. I wish I could say they did."

A horse quietly nickered. The sun would be coming up in a few hours and Deacon knew it, even if Joe had lost track of the time.

"Why don't you walk back to camp, Joe? I'll tend the remuda so you can get a little sleep. This ol' rock ain't much of a bunk," Deacon said.

"I can't let you do that. Don't you ever sleep?"

"Sure I do. I just sleep different than most folks. I just close one eye at a time. That way I can sleep in the saddle and keep right on riding."

"Aww come on. You're funnin' me," Joe said.

"Go on and get some sleep, Joe. I'll be along to get you near day break," Deacon said.

Joe got up and headed in the direction of camp.

Indeed it *had* been a very long time since Deacon had had a full and sound night of sleep. He'd pretty much given up hope that he ever would again.

As daybreak neared, Johnny slept fitfully near the low campfire. A couple of hours earlier, he and Ben had returned to camp. Ben had led their horses out to the remuda, surprised to find Deacon with the horses, rather than Joe.

It would be a slow start to the day given that most of the men were still in town, enjoying their last hours before heading north. This fact was one Emmett hoped he wouldn't regret. Too late now, he thought as he rolled up his bedroll, thinking it would be just about time for Hucks to be getting the morning meal started. He picked up his saddle and carried it in the direction of the remuda. He always tried to be the first one mounted in the mornings, and this day would not be a difficult one on which to achieve that aspiration.

On the way out to the horses, he was met by Deacon on his way back to camp.

"Mornin', Emmett."

"Mornin', Deacon. You sleep out here?"

"Maybe a little. I figured it was gettin' nigh on light enough to leave the horses and get to camp. I staked out the bay mare for you, 'less you want another'un."

"Much obliged. She'll do just fine."

"Joe knew she was due for you to ride, and told me so."

"He's a good boy," Emmett allowed.

"Provin' out pretty good, if you ask me," Deacon replied.

"That he surely seems to be," Emmett said. "The camp is quiet, except for Hucks. He'll roust 'em out once he's got the morning meal ready."

Emmett nodded and resumed his walk, and so did Deacon, arriving in camp to find Ben and Joe still sleeping near the fire.

Deacon sat down next to his saddle. It occurred to him that he couldn't remember the last time he took off his boots. He picked up a lariat he'd been working on earlier and resumed braiding it. He'd made so many over the years that it was almost second nature to him and he could practically do it with his eyes closed. He braided and watched the fire, listening to Hucks go about his work, preparing the morning meal and keeping an occasional eye on Johnny, whose sleep grew more and more animated and troubled.

Joe and Ben both stirred at the sound of Johnny's restlessness. They both came fully awake at the foreign sound of Johnny's fitful sleep, and began watching him as they rose and put away their bedrolls.

Emmett rode into camp, dismounted and tied off the bay mare to the makeshift hitching post that Joe had made before he went to sleep.

"Where's Delbert? And Luke?" he asked, assessing the scene.

"They're still in town. Delbert is looking after Luke. When Johnny and I headed back out, he was trying to get him out of the Bella Donna in one piece, and without a night in jail," Ben replied.

"Some things never change," Emmett said. He looked over at Johnny, whose sleep was growing more and more troubled. "What's the story with him?" he asked.

"Said he needed to sleep it off," Ben said.

"Well gettin' drunk and raisin' a bit of a ruckus is part of it. Ft. Worth is the last fun there'll be before we get to Abilene."

"He wasn't drunk. Just drinking," Ben said. "He kept mumbling something about not being able to see through the fog. I thought it strange. It was a dark night, but there certainly wasn't any fog."

Emmett nodded in acknowledgement.

Johnny stirred and moaned loudly in his sleep. Deacon looked up from his braiding.

"How come you're back already?" Emmett asked Ben.

"Delbert thought it best I head on back to camp before things got out of hand. Luke was…"

"Bein' Luke," Deacon interjected.

Johnny jerked violently as he slept, suddenly enough for Emmett's horse to take notice.

"They're here. They're here!" Johnny said. "There's too damn many of 'em!"

Joe watched Johnny with pity, tears welling up in his eyes.

Johnny suddenly let out a blood curdling scream, startling the camp, the remuda and the cattle.

"Oh, God. Oh, God. Did it go clean through? Please let it be clean through! Ambulance!" Johnny cried. "Oh please God, please don't let me die here. Oh, God no."

Johnny whimpered pitifully.

"Mama."

His breathing became very heavy.

"Mama."

"Mama!" he screamed.

Johnny clutched his side, in apparent pain and distress. Ben moved toward Johnny and was going to attempt to comfort him.

"Leave him be. That's a dream he'll have to see through to the end," Emmett said.

Johnny's body went still.

"Pa told me that most men cry for their mama when they think they're gonna die," Joe said.

"That damn war was hell on everybody," Emmett said, shaking his head.

"Pa always said that even the men that came home never really came home, not all the way anyhow," Joe said.

He looked at Johnny for a long moment. The site of a grown man in the prime of his life, shaking, shivering, fearing his own death still, if only in his dreams, brought profound feelings of sympathy to Joe. He longed for a way to comfort Johnny, to let him know that he could be among friends, if he wanted to be. But all he could muster was a blank stare through misty eyes.

Deacon looked blankly at him as well, unmoved, then returned to his braiding.

"Ben, you and Johnny take the swing today," Emmett said. "Javier is due back today sometime...with good news I hope."

Seeing that Hucks was well on his way to having the morning meal ready, he thought it time to get the men in motion.

"Hucks, time to rouse these boys out and get 'em fed.

It's a slow start to the day, but we'll need to make some progress today anyhow," he said, "Delbert'll be back by and by with Luke, and we'll get this herd headed true north 'fore mid-day. Deacon, you stay on point. That's where you'll do us the most good."

"Yes, sir. That I'll do," Deacon said.

CHAPTER TWELVE

TOUGH TRAIL

IT WAS PROVING TO BE a slow, leisurely breakfast, unusually good-natured given the state that some of the men were in. Delbert and Luke had arrived from town while everyone was still eating. Delbert looked quite tired, which was understandable given the difficult babysitting duty he had served. Luke, on the other hand, looked like he had been run over by a team of mules driven by the devil himself. Fortunately for them, they hadn't missed the morning meal and a plate of beans and sow belly did them both much good.

Joe approached Hucks, his empty plate in hand.

"Mr. Hucks, do you think I can have another biscuit and maybe a few more beans?" he asked.

"Nice to see you fattenin' up a might," Hucks replied, as he dolloped a big spoon full of beans onto Joe's plate.

Joe smile broadly and said, "Thank you, sir."

Joe returned to the circle of men sitting near the small coffee fire and sat down next to Deacon, who was just about finished braiding the rope he had been working on.

The men were having some fun at Luke's expense, though he was in no mood whatsoever to cotton it.

"What do you mean you lost your pistol?" Delbert asked.

"It's just gone. I had it and then I didn't have it," Luke said.

"Are you sure you didn't use it to ante up for another poker hand when I had my back turned?"

"I'm sure as sure can be. I'd never be stupid enough to do that again," Luke replied.

"I wouldn't put money on that," Johnny added. He'd awoken in a quieter mood than usual, but not at all a sullen one.

"Well young Ben here's got himself a real fine piece of hardware. If you ask nice, he might even be willing to sell it to you," Delbert said, grinning slyly.

Luke had not noticed the pistol ensconced in Ben's belt.

"Hey! That's mine! You stole my pistol!" Luke yelled.

"Oh, spare us, for Pete's sake. That boy's probably the reason you're sittin' here with us right now. Saved you a killin', sure as the sun rose this morning," Johnny said, his tone flat, cold and matter-of-fact.

"Of course it's yours. I only took it for safekeeping. You ought to know me well enough by now to know that I wouldn't steal from anyone. Here you go," Ben said as he pulled the pistol from his belt and handed it to Luke, holding it by the barrel and offering him the pistol grip.

"Thanks," Luke replied, snatching the pistol from Ben's hand with a healthy dose of indignation. As he holstered the weapon he paused reflectively for a moment. "I mean… thanks," Luke said, this time with a touch of warmth.

"You're welcome," Ben replied with a smile.

"Well you know what they say about a fool and his money. I reckon they'd say the same about a fool and his pistol," Hucks chimed in, chuckling to himself with a small measure of self-satisfaction.

Emmett was sitting at a makeshift desk near the wagon that he'd fashioned with a wide piece of lumber over two barrels. He reached down and into the saddlebag that was on the ground at his feet and removed a small sheaf of papers, a pen, and a carefully wrapped inkwell. He gently smoothed out a piece of paper and began to write.

"Javier," Delbert said.

Emmett looked up from the paper and gazed northward, knowing that would be the direction from which Javier would be returning. He squinted and saw in the distance a rider slumped over his horse. The horse was walking slowly and gingerly.

"I'd better ride out to meet him," Delbert said.

"Probably a good idea," Emmett replied.

Hucks was fishing around in the back of his wagon and found an extra canteen, which he dipped in the water barrel, filling up quickly and handing it to Delbert.

"This'll do him some good."

Delbert saddled his horse, mounted and kicked his horse into a gallop in the direction of Javier.

"I don't like the looks of that," Hucks said.

"Me neither," Emmett replied.

The men watched as Delbert met up with Javier and gave him some water. They continued to walk slowly towards camp. As they approached, Hucks grabbed a large ladle hanging on the side of the water barrel.

Javier and Delbert reached camp and dismounted. Joe

took Javier's horse as well as Delbert's. Hucks handed Javier the ladle filled with water. He took it and drank most of it down quickly, leaving a small amount which he slowly drizzled down the back of his neck.

"From the looks of your mount, I expect you went a lot further than you planned," Emmett said, glad to see Javier revived somewhat.

"She's spent but sound I think," Joe offered.

Emmett nodded in acknowledgement.

"Si. A lot further. Eighty, maybe a hundred miles," Javier answered.

The look on Emmett's face left no doubt as to the depth of his worry and concern.

"How bad is it?" he asked.

Javier paused a moment before replying. "Bad."

"Tell me."

He looked around at the men who were all looking at him, wondering and worrying.

"I was about to write a letter to Mr. Callaway on another matter, so I should include word on what's ahead of us so he'll be prepared."

"There's good water two days ahead. After that, nothing until we make the Red River, not that I could find anyway. That's a good sixty or seventy miles beyond," Javier said.

Hucks grunted his disapproval.

"Herd just ahead of us had to turn back to our next water, so I don't know if they'll even be gone by the time we get there. Could be a mud hole by then," Javier continued.

"That's the Four Sixes. Roscoe will head east 'fore he heads 'em back north. Heck, with any luck, we may even beat him to Abilene. He ain't exactly the hurryin' sort. But he'll likely be gone alright."

Emmett scanned slowly around the camp, looking each man in the eye.

"We're gonna need some luck, men. And for those of you who follow the Good Book, you might toss a prayer up to the Good Lord."

This was one of those moments when the individual and collective risks of the enterprise focused their minds. The slow, tedious drudgery of each day strung together sometimes made it easy to forget the danger, at times. Moments like that were the stark reminders of the enormity of the task, the importance of each man's part on the drive.

"I sent for three more barrels so we could take extra at least for the boys if not some of the horses. I'll be pickin' 'em up when I lay in supplies on my way through town. I'd better get moving. Since breakfast was late, I figure the boys can eat some jerk beef in the saddle for the mid-day meal. I'll travel well ahead of the herd and have an early supper ready for them," Hucks added.

Emmett leveled his gaze squarely at Hucks, knowing his propensity to fall into the bottle, often on inopportune occasions. "Don't get sidetracked, Hucks. There's dead serious business in front of us."

"Not a drop, Emmett. I swear it."

Javier's estimation of the distance to water proved to be accurate, and the herd reached a large, slow moving stream two days later. To call it a river would've been overly generous, but it was wide and shallow, with somewhat steep banks on either side. This made for safer crossing, by preventing any cattle getting bogged down in the mud, or at least minimizing the chances of it at any rate.

The Four Sixes cattle were long gone and the stream, though apparently well below its previous levels, was more than adequate to service the Bar Nothin' herd. Knowing there would be at least a week of slow, hot, hard travel before they would reach the Red River, Emmett allowed the herd to linger a half day longer than they normally would have. He hoped the extended time would give the herd, as well as the horses and men, a chance to build strength before they resumed northward.

Three days after they left the stream, Emmett was sad to know that his instincts had been correct.

Not two hours after the morning meal, the sun shone so hot as to render a man incapable of judging far-off distances. The glimmer of the heat radiating from the ground was a stark reminder of the desolate, hardscrabble nature of that part of the country. As the day wore on, and the intensity of the sun grew ever stronger, the slow pace of the herd grew even slower.

For good or ill, the wind stayed quiet. Emmett had mixed feelings about it. On the one hand, a breeze would freshen the dead air that seemed to stifle every breath the men and animals drew. On the other hand, too much wind would kick up a cloud of sand that would make breathing and seeing difficult.

At mid-morning, on the fourth day their luck ran out. From the south and west a strong and sustained wind started to blow. It blew so hard that the stinging sand threatened to peel the hide and hair off the cattle and horses. The men covered up every exposed area they could, but their leathery hands were no match for the needle like sensation of the blowing sand. With hats pulled down low, and eyes squinted and almost shut, the men could barely see well enough to work, but just barely.

Delbert rode up ahead to check on Joe and the remuda. As he approached, he saw Joe on the ground next to a fallen horse.

"You alright, Joe?" he asked.

Joe looked up, his face caked with sand from the tears that were streaming down his face.

"I can't get him up, Delbert. He won't get up," he said in anguish.

"Aww, heck, that's Chaw. What happened?" Delbert asked.

"I don't know. He just fell. The horses were all moving fine and then, he just went down."

Delbert's heart sunk. He knew the little horse was going no further, and frankly, had his doubts when Emmett agreed to allow him to follow the remuda. He also knew that this would be a brutal blow to Joe, his loyalty and allegiance to Chaw being born on their safe flight from home.

"He's not gonna get up, is he?" Joe asked, knowing the answer already.

"I'm afraid not, son. He's got a big heart, this little horse, but the sad fact is that not every horse is stout enough to make this kind of trip."

Joe tried to wipe his tears, but the sand only made the tears flow more strongly.

"You stay with the other horses and try to keep 'em together. I'll take care of Chaw," Delbert said, pulling his pistol out of its holster.

"No. Please don't," Joe said, reaching his hand out to Delbert.

"Joe, I have to. It would be cruel to just let him die slow."

"I know."

Joe paused and looked down at the little brown horse. "I have to be the one. Give me your pistol and let me do it."

Delbert slowly handed Joe the pistol. In that moment of sadness, he felt a strange, faint feeling of happiness. He now knew what he had suspected about Joe. He knew that Joe's love and compassion for the horses in his care was deep and genuine, and he knew that Joe was a man inside, even though his physical stature didn't yet fit the description.

"Make it quick and then get the horses gathered back up. I have to go find Emmett."

"I will," Joe said, nodding with a sniff of his nose.

The wind began to subside. A blessing that would come with a curse. Not long after, the sun shone brightly again, hot and strong enough to melt metal, or so it seemed to the men.

Delbert finally found Emmett, who'd been helping out on the drag, doing his part to keep the drive moving.

"Havin' a devil of a time keeping them moving. They're trying to scatter and double back," Delbert said.

"They're trying to head back to last water," Emmett replied.

"Should we rest 'em?" Delbert asked.

"No. If we do, we'll never get 'em moving again, at least not moving north."

"What do you want to do?"

Emmett pondered for a moment.

"Have to keep moving. All night."

"The boys've been in the saddle for a day and half now," Delbert said.

"I know. So've we. If we can keep moving tonight, we have a decent chance at making water by late tomorrow," Emmett replied. "If we can hold 'em together."

"If," Delbert added.

"Move Javi up to point and drop Deacon back on drag. I'll stay back here too," Emmett said. "Keep pushing."

"Yes, sir," Delbert said as he headed off to make his way up to the front of the herd.

Deacon pulled out his pistol and fired near the head of the lead steer. He noted Delbert's arrival.

"Lead steer's gone blind," Deacon said.

"Thirst blind," Delbert replied.

"If I shoot near him every little while, I can keep him pointed north, but I don't know how much longer that'll work," Deacon said. "The rest are gettin' blind too and ain't much for followin'."

"Emmett says if we can keep them moving all night we have a chance to make water by late day tomorrow."

Delbert looked at the lead steer and some of the other steers near them.

"They'll get their sight back after they drink," he said.

"If we make it," Deacon said. He paused for a moment in thought. "I need to swap mounts," he said.

"Alright. Find Javi and tell him I said to join me up here on point. Then you can change mounts," Delbert said. "Emmett wants you on drag with him and Johnny."

Deacon headed off. Delbert cussed to himself that the flies, swarming and persistent, had taken the place of the sand as the plague of the moment.

CHAPTER THIRTEEN

RUSTLERS

THE HERD MADE IT TO the Red River at dusk the next day, having traveled more slowly as each hour trudged by. The men were exhausted, as were the horses and cattle. Javier had found a good place for them to ford the river, and most of the cattle crossed after a long drink and a bit of rest. There were a few that were more than happy to linger, however. That meant that, as Joe and Delbert gathered up the horses, Deacon and Johnny were forced to round up the stragglers. So, with the rest of the herd happily on the move north, there were some that needed a bit of gentle, or in some cases, not so gentle, persuasion.

"I'm gonna take the horses up ahead," Delbert called to the others, with the horses ready for the forward march. "Joe, you stay with Deacon and Johnny to help 'em get the last of the strays gathered."

"Yes, sir," Joe said, in serious fashion. He turned to take direction from Deacon, fully prepared to do his part to get the last of the herd moving again. But, a second later, he was looking over his shoulder. "Delbert?"

"Yeah?"

"What about my remuda?"

The innocent question just served to further endear Joe to his superior. He hid his smile, keeping the tone as serious as the young man's question had been. "They're in good hands, Joe. I'll look after 'em 'til you get up there." As an afterthought, he added, "I'll leave 'em for you to bed down."

No longer fearing the loss of his treasured role, the boy smiled and nodded. "Thank you."

With the decision made, Delbert gave the signal and the horses started to move, kicking up a fair amount of dust, despite a relatively slow pace.

"C'mon Joe," Deacon called out, having witnessed the scene, "We gotta get these cows movin' if we're gonna get you back in time to bed down those horses. They won't need a lot of pushin'. They like to be with the herd. Just get on the outside of 'em and urge 'em toward the bunch up ahead."

Deacon was right, and with a little effort, they had quickly gathered the small number back into a bunch and were ready to begin moving toward the larger herd. They had only gone a short distance when Johnny's horse whinnied and wheeled around quickly, clearly startled by something. Johnny started to correct the horse's course, but Deacon stilled him with a hand gesture. Joe looked on, suddenly feeling Deacon's tension. A moment later, four horses could be made out on the horizon, moving at a good clip toward the recently gathered herd. Without a word, Deacon started the forward process once again, choosing, it seemed, to ignore the approaching men. Joe, thought, correctly, that it wasn't so much ignoring as it was an effort to move as close as possible to the big herd ahead. It wouldn't do much good, though. These stragglers might have been relatively easy to round up, and they might have been willingly moving in the correct direction, but they were not going to be hurried. Before long, the four unknown cowboys had come close enough to cause Deacon to stop all forward momentum.

"Thank you boys for gatherin' up our strays," said the apparent leader of the group, a smirk pulling at the corners of his mouth.

Joe watched, his horse standing just behind those of Deacon and Johnny. He saw that Johnny had slightly lowered his head, breaking eye contact with the threat and allowing the brim of his hat to cover most his face. It was quickly clear why he had no wish to show his identity to the new arrivals.

"Well as I live and breathe, ain't you a sight, Johnny. Been years," another of the men called out, making it clear that he considered Johnny to be his inferior.

Deacon fought the urge to make a comment about his lack of surprise at there being a connection between these men and the one who had been his nemesis throughout the days of the drive.

"These here cattle belong to the Bar Nothin'," he said instead.

The first of the intruders spoke up once more, answering the claim, "You'll keep your mouth shut, unless you want trouble, boy," and dropped his hand to the pistol resting at his hip. He made no move to draw, but his lip pulled up, taking his expression from a smirk to a snarl. The teeth that could be seen between his lips were stained and partially rotten from the enjoyment of too much tobacco over the years.

At the word, Deacon's shoulders visibly stiffened. Feeling the stress of its rider, Deacon's horse pawed the ground with nervous energy. "I ain't no boy."

The claim fell on deaf ears, as the second rider turned, once more, to Johnny. "How'd you end up on the trail with an uppity colored and a runt kid? Thought you'd turn out to be more cowboy than that."

Rather than answering the question, which intended harm to the whole crew, Johnny asked his own question. "I remember you, but I don't remember your name."

Visibly insulted at not being remembered, the other man nudged another of his group, "Well, don't that just beat all," and then turning his glare back to Johnny, "We served together. We bled together, but then, I wouldn't be expectin' you and this gatherin' to care nothin' about that."

"Some things are best left in the past," responded Johnny, and Joe wondered if he weren't saying it as much to himself as he was to the rustler.

Perhaps hearing an apology in the statement, Deacon claimed the silence. "Joe, why don't you ease on over to the other side of that ridge? I thought I saw one or two more head over there. We don't want to take no chance of losing any if we can help it." He said it all without looking back at the boy, and Joe hesitated, turning his gaze from Johnny to Deacon and back again several times before doing as he was told.

Not wasting any time, once the boy started his horse at a trot away from the group, the rustler repeated once more, "Like I said, thank ya for gatherin' up our cattle."

Deacon, holding the reins on his temper even tighter than the ones in his hand, glared at the man, "And, like I said, them there are Bar Nothin' cattle. The brand's as clear as day."

"Ours is the Aught brand and it looks like you branded the bar right over it. That's something a thievin' Sambo would do," The man replied with another evil smirk — a smirk that Deacon would have been more than pleased to smack off his face.

The other, with a angry chuckle, turned once more to his former brother in arms.

"Who do these cattle belong to, Johnny?" An awkward, menacing silence surrounded them.

Deacon jumped in, nervous anger overwhelming him, but not enough to allow him to overlook the threat.

"Look here, you're welcome to take any range cattle there is here. We won't claim 'em."

He looked to Johnny, trying to tell him, without words, to let the fight go. Then, looking back to the instigators, he added, "that's my one and only peace offering."

"I don't need no peace offering, boy. Not from you or any of your kind."

The second rustler, not about to let the matter drop, hammered on Johnny once more, "Who do they belong to, Johnny? I say they're branded Aught. You're a hero of the Confederacy, and I'm askin' you. Whose cattle are they?" Feeling like a rabbit caught in a fatal trap, Johnny just turned his eyes from the man to Deacon and back again.

Deacon's temper started to shift, as the confusion in Johnny's face became increasingly clear. "Yeah, Johnny Reb," he said turning on the man who he never wanted to work with in the first place, "Who do they belong to?" Before the words had even fully cleared his lips, all hands were resting on pistols.

Even more conflicted, Johnny was slow to form words, "you heard him…"

The statement was cut short by the sound of Joe's voice, "Deacon, there weren't no more cattle around there," spoken with confusion, and nervousness. It was a justified anxiety, and one felt by all who stood there. Tired of the back and forth, concerned that reinforcements were on the way, a third member of the rustler's crew became trigger happy. He drew, aimed and fired. Joe's eyes visibly grew in size, time seemingly standing still as Johnny looked on. The dust hadn't yet settled from the horse's hooves, despite the fact that it now sat still beneath the boy. The sun, behind his head, put the still too thin, cowboy-in-training in a near silhouette, and Johnny found himself wishing that he could reach out and catch that bullet. Instead, before he could see that it had flew just enough left of Joe to leave him uninjured, Johnny had turned his own pistol on the intruders, filled with hatred for them, and for his own indecision.

As bullets flew, horses spun, whinnied and pawed the ground, turning their riders right and left in the cloud raised from the earth below. And, despite his training, despite his time fighting for the Confederacy, Johnny found in those panicked moments that he had never felt such a need to defend a cause as he did after seeing the bullet whiz toward the boy's head.

Deacon couldn't see much in the cloud that had risen up

around them, but it was as if the dust cleared just so he would see the moment that Johnny's bullet tore into the chest of the man that he had served with. Johnny's face was not one of regret as he spared a quick glance for his fellow cowboy. It was one of retribution and acceptance. With two of his men in a heap on the ground, their horses nervously rearing and clamoring about, the leader of the rustlers did a quick about-face. He gave his horse a sharp kick with both spurs in a mighty effort to get away. Deacon brought his pistol up, taking careful aim and squeezing off two shots, one of which winged the retreating rustler. The distance grew too great for him to try a third shot, so he decided to save the bullet.

Feeling a burning sensation, like Hucks had built a campfire in his lap, Deacon looked down to see the red streaming from the hole in his chaps. Not wanting to know how bad the wound really was, he pulled his eyes from the offending sight and he lifted them to see the stunned expressions of Joe and Johnny.

"You're hit," Johnny said, as if it was only beginning to make sense to him. Joe's face, already devoid of much of its natural color went one shade whiter as he looked down to Deacon's leg.

Deacon, swaying with the effort of holding his mount, smiled at the boy. "It ain't nothin' I can't handle, Joe. It was in and out." He scanned his surroundings, seeing the backs of the recent adversaries fading as they approached the horizon. The site of the two dead men was a grim reminder of the finality of it. It had been a very long time since he'd seen death this close, and as used to it as Deacon had grown in the past, it wasn't something he wanted to see again.

"All the same, let's have a look," responded Johnny, jumping down from his horse. He handed the reins to Joe, which caused the boy to look away from Deacon's leg.

"Take the horses, will ya?" Johnny said. Having a purpose to serve, some of the color returned to Joe's face, and he took hold of all three sets of reins.

"Should I...?" He asked, looking to the dead rustlers, and then to their horses. Johnny nodded, and said, "String 'em along." Joe took up the two additional sets of reins and, tying each to the saddle horn of the other horses, led all of them a short distance away from the bodies.

Deacon's dismount was far from the usual. A hiss of air rushed past his teeth as the searing pain shot up his limb on the impact of hitting solid Earth. The sound called Joe's attention back to the wound, at which he stared for several seconds. The look of fear was replaced with one of curiosity.

With more frustration than he would normally aim at the boy, Deacon snapped, "What's the matter, Joe? Ain't you never seen blood before?"

Shrinking in embarrassment, Joe looked away before responding, "Well, yeah. But, I ain't never seen a colored man's blood." Both the men look at him, as he pointed to Johnny's arm, where a bullet had grazed the skin, ripping the sleeve. "Your blood's red, same as Johnny's."

Deacon, calming in the presence of the boy's innocence, shook his head, "'course. What color'd you expect it to be?"

"Hadn't thought on it much, I s'pose," Joe responded as Johnny began fashioning makeshift bandages for torn strips of cloth from his shirt.

"You been hit too," Deacon said to the other man, "you know," he continued, lowering his eyes before raising them again to look straight into Johnny's, "you ain't gotta do this."

Johnny, after holding the gaze for a moment, lowered his eyes to his task, "Ain't my first field dressing."

Joe watched on as the man showcased his level of expertise with such matters. The strips of cloth were soon set aside, and as Johnny cut away the fabric of the breeches, he looked in Deacon's face again.

"You don't think I'd just let you sit there and bleed to death?" With the pants pushed away from the wound, Johnny was able to apply pressure, his own blood running down his forearm, and eventually joining the river of Deacon's.

"Deacon?" Joe asked, looking on. "Johnny?" When both men tilted their faces up to him, Joe swallowed forcibly, looking back to the red streaming down Deacon's leg. "Does this mean y'all are blood brothers now?"

As the silence dragged on between the three, Joe let some slack in the horses' lines and lowered himself to sit cross legged, just feet from the men. Johnny continued the ministrations to Deacon's wound, binding the leg with the strips of cloth, until all was cleanly covered.

After several minutes had passed, he looked up into Deacon's face for a moment, "I think maybe it does, Joe," he said without breaking eye contact, receiving a slight nod in return.

CHAPTER FOURTEEN

VISITORS

ROSA GAZED OUT AT THE hazy horizon. With hands on her hips, she bent backward stretching the tight muscles of her lower back, and enjoyed the sight of the sun climbing above the haze. A whinny from the corral reminded her of her mission. She made her way to the large corral near the house and swung the large gate open, standing out of the way to avoid the rush of hooves.

As soon as they were in the pasture, the horses lowered their heads, grazing as was their nature. Her mind traveled to her husband, and what he might be doing at the moment. Those horses were going to secure them an enjoyable, profitable life together, but only if he returned to her.

The thoughts weighed heavy on her heart, but still she smiled as the horses moved a few feet at a time, each searching for the perfect patch of grass. It was the loud thump from the porch that called her attention away from the horses. Momentarily startled, she turned her attention to Ellie, the door still reverberating from the impact of slamming shut.

"Sorry," Ellie called, burdened by the weight of the

large rug from the main room of the house. "I didn't mean to startle you."

Rosa waved the apology away and started to move away, toward the chickens' coop after seeing that Ellie had successfully thrown the rug over the line. As she walked away, she could hear the rhythmic beat of the beater hitting the rug. She laughed lightly when she heard Ellie sneeze in the cloud of dust she was releasing into the air. They never could beat the rugs without sneezing.

Upon reaching the coops, Rosa shooed the hens and rooster into the run and doled out the food. A loud crow was her thanks, which she figured was better than the usual attack on her boots. When the chickens were happily scratching and pecking, she gathered the eggs that had accumulated since the day before, placing them into the little basket that she had fashioned for herself, and then began shoveling the bedding from the coop before she filled it with clean straw. With the basket gently swinging in her hand, she headed for the house.

Ellie, inside the house, had set her broom aside and moved to the makeshift cradle. The sight of Jeremiah sleeping after having had a good feeding was something she could never tire of. The child might not have had the greatest start, but he was safe, happy and healthy here. She reached her hand in, gently running the tip of her finger over his small belly. Hearing Rosa climbing the porch steps, though, she guiltily hurried out the door and to the rain barrel. Without saying a word, she handed the ladle filled with cool water to her friend.

"Good number of eggs. The girls have started laying again," she said after happily accepting the drink. Three of their hens had hatched a brood of chicks each. For more than nine weeks, their egg counts had been extremely low, which made baking a challenge. Ellie smiled and refilled the ladle, handing it, once again to Rosa, who took another big sip and wiped her brow. The flat land stretched far beyond them and she looked out to the farthest distances for the second time that morning, the sadness and worry returning to her heart and to her face.

"You all right, Rosa? Figured the eggs would have put a smile on your face." Rosa nodded, though the smile didn't reach her eyes as she sat down in the nearest chair. She signaled with a slight movement of her head for Ellie to join her. Ellie gladly accepted the invitation, and dropped into the adjacent chair.

"I have lived in South Texas my whole life and somehow I still can't get used to this heat," Rosa answered, as if this would explain the cloud of gloom that had followed her around for days.

Ellie eyed her inquisitively for a long while before looking away, and to the horses, which still grazed contentedly in the pasture. After several minutes had passed, and the ache had eased from her shoulders, she slumped back in the chair and focused back on the woman beside her. "Does seem like this summer is worse than usual."

"I think I agree," was the muttered response from Rosa, who seemed engrossed on the far pastures. Ellie could see the clouds in her eyes, knowing full well that Rosa's thoughts were far away. They were very likely with the man who had spent many years working on those very fields, speaking to the horses in the pastures, and doing the hard labor that left the women's backs sore.

Just when Ellie thought the conversation would go no further, Rosa's eyes cleared and her face brightened. "I have no right to complain. We have shade, and plenty to eat and drink. You're right, you know. I should be smiling about the eggs, thinking about what we might bake for ourselves. We even have a soft bed at night, and we got each other's company." She too sat back in her chair, collapsing, as if under the weight of the world. "My poor Javi," the sadness of her tone broke Ellie's heart, "He's got none of these things."

Tears threatened to choke Ellie. She fought back the memories of feeling exactly that way about her own man, the man who would never have any of those comforts, that conversation, the warm bed again. "Please don't worry, Rosa. Javier will be fine. He'll come back to you. He loves you too much not to."

"You know that that isn't always how it happens," she said. "*You* know," she repeated with a heavy emphasis. "How am I not to worry?" Ellie stared at her friend. She wanted so badly to lie, to deny the truth behind Rosa's words, to make her friend feel better, but she couldn't.

Ellie had to look away, saying only, "You are right, I suppose."

The two sat in silence, the thoughts of chores to be done chased away by the even more common worry. After a while, Rosa spoke, as if in mid-thought and as much to herself as to her friend, "…and Javi is a scout. Days and nights alone. Hoping his horse doesn't go lame and leave him to die in the hot sun. Hoping he can avoid bands of Comanches. Hoping he can find water for the herd. Hoping…" She choked on a sob, fighting to get the rest out, but only succeeding in a trickle of a whisper, "hoping for a son." Tears silently ran down her face. Ellie stood from her chair and then dropped to her knees in front of Rosa, taking the other woman's hand in her own.

"Oh Rosa," she said, holding tight to the hand. "Hope is the way. It's God's way to show us His Grace."

Rosa took her hand back, placing it momentarily on Ellie's arm and then bringing it to her face to wipe away the tears. "I know."

"If you have hope, He will show you a way." Rosa looked down into Ellie's face, letting the words sink in and allowing the sadness to drain from her body. Suddenly, her face brightened, causing Ellie to smile nervously.

"Yes. Yes maybe He will," Rosa said.

Ellie's smile fell, and she cocked her head in confusion. "What?"

Rosa patted her arm again and then helped her to her feet and back into the chair. Still standing, she looked at Ellie and then away, walking to the porch rail. She held tight and without turning back said, "I want to ask you something."

Ellie's voice was anything but confident. "What?"

"You know how important it is to Javier to have a son," Rosa began, turning back with a look of determination.

"Uh... I think so," Ellie responded, adding in a somewhat guilty manner, "I couldn't help but overhear some of your talks."

Ignoring the apology in the words, Rosa kept on going, her idea taking a more concrete form as she spoke, "and you know that we have been trying for a number of years to start a family, right?"

"Yes," Ellie answered, searching Rosa's face for explanation. After a moment, she said, "Rosa, what are you driving at?"

"Do you..." A blush rose in Rosa's face. She looked away, but not before Ellie saw the blood rush to her cheeks. "Do you find Javier to be an attractive man?" When she didn't receive an immediate answer, Rosa turned back to her friend and saw the understanding suddenly register on her face.

"Oh no. No, no, no," Ellie stammered, shaking her head, and then seeing the hurt in Rosa's eyes, she corrected herself, "I mean, yes, Javier... I mean, no... I haven't ... I mean... I can't."

"Ellie. You're a widow. You're young..." Rosa swallowed hard, "You're fertile."

"Rosa," Ellie stood and walked to her friend, placing a hand on her back, as they both looked out to the distance. "I can't, Rosa. You know I can't."

"Just... Just think about it," Rosa responded, a plea in her expression.

The awkward discomfort dissolved in short order between Ellie and Rosa, as the need to complete chores occupied too much of their time to allow their thoughts to linger on the topic. A week had passed and neither woman was dwelling on the idea any longer. They worked side by side in the garden, pulling the pesky weeds that seemed intent on choking out the vegetable plants. Ellie looked up into Rosa's face, which appeared devoid of color.

"Are you ill, Rosa?" she asked, peering into the glassy

eyes of the other woman. Rosa shook her head. She knelt in the soil between rows of plants.

"I don't feel well at all. I'm so tired."

"Let's get you inside," Ellie said, feeling a sudden urgency. "I need to nurse Jeremiah anyway," she added, looking around her and then gesturing to the plants, "This will wait."

Rosa started to shake her head, but Ellie wouldn't let her. She reached down and grabbed her friend's hand, helping her to her feet. Feeling a wave of dizziness overtake her, Rosa reluctantly agreed. As she took the first few steps toward the house, her feet felt as though they were made of lead.

Ellie looked on, with worry, to where Rosa slept. She had managed to get her into the house, but the poor woman's face had drained of all color upon reaching the front porch. By the time they were through the door, it was clear that she wasn't going to make it any further on her feet and Ellie reached out in an effort to catch her. The force sent them both to the floor. Rosa's unconscious form was heavy, but working on the ranch had made Ellie strong. She was able to get her into the bedroom and onto the straw-filled mattress. Now, sprawled out on the bed, Rosa slumbered and her once pale face was red with fever.

Rosa mumbled as she returned to consciousness. Ellie dipped a cloth into a nearby bucket of water and wrung it out, bringing the cool cloth back to her friend's head, watching her eyes slowly flutter open.

"Feeling better?" Ellie asked, as Rosa carefully raised

herself up on her elbows, as if trying to get a sense of her surroundings, trying to make sense of how she wound up on her bed.

She nodded, "Si. Quite a bit. I don't know what happened," she looked at Ellie, confused before sliding her legs over the side of the bed. "Out of nowhere… I just felt like I had to sleep… or something."

Ellie smiled at her, eyes gleaming. "Such a thing happens sometimes."

Rosa was sweeping the porch, which seemed endlessly dusty, thanks to the recent winds that stirred the ground, making it look as it if was a living thing, constantly roiling. But keeping the porch swept seemed to be the thing that required all the time in between their many other chores. She shook her head watching the swirls of earth as they rose, settled, and rose again. She didn't see the blurred silhouette of three men standing several hundred yards in the distance, though they intently watched her. Thinking to herself that her current undertaking was a futile task, she swept a little faster and raised her voice to call for her friend in the house.

"Ellie, are you almost finished nursing? I need your help finishing up out here so I can bring in the horses." There was no answer, and so she swept for another couple of seconds, pushing a pile of dust over the edge and watched it fall before calling again, "Ellie?" When, again, she received no answer, she placed the broom against the rail, and headed for the door. It banged slightly behind her as she entered, as the spring caught the weight and called it back to the door frame. "Ellie?"

She walked through the doorway and found her friend, with the baby in her arms. Little Jeremiah's eyelids lowered and snapped open, only to fall once more, as he lost his battle against sleep. Ellie held a finger to her lips and smiled up at her friend. Rosa was about to return the smile when she heard the nervous whinnies of the horses in the pasture just beyond the window. Both women tensed, visibly, and Rosa glanced once more at the baby before grabbing the shotgun that they kept loaded by the door.

She grabbed the door handle and pulled it before she saw him. His face was so close that she could smell his putrid breath and see how deeply the jagged knife scar ran across his cheek.

She didn't have time to react. He grabbed the shotgun out of her hands and threw her to the ground. All that she could comprehend was the feeling of the insides shifting in her head as it slammed against the floor. Hearing the impact, Ellie came running, with the baby still firmly in her arms. She grabbed the pistol from the table and took aim at the man who had accosted her friend. Jeremiah's eyes popped open again, and he seemed to take in the scene, just as the man's two partners did, having rounded the corner. Before the baby could let loose a scream in protest to being waken, two more pistols were drawn and aimed at Ellie.

Paying no respect to either of the women, or the child, one of the men turned to the first, "Mother lode, just like you said. Two hundred fifty, maybe three hundred head. Good horses too." The leader, and the man who had pushed Rosa took a moment to let the words sink in. He glanced away from Ellie and turned his gaze on Rosa, where she still lay at his feet.

"Well now, where might your menfolk be?"

Rosa wasn't about to give in, to play weak, despite the menacing grin that grew on the intruder's face. She glared up at him, trying to ignore the pain radiating through her as a result of being thrown so forcefully. Pushing up on both elbows, she spit the words out. "On the way back from town. I expect them any time now."

The menacing grin grew larger and evolved into a full-fledged laugh. The other two men, standing just behind him joined in, chuckling at her obvious lie.

"Now we both know that ain't true, don't we?" The leader asked, gently moving the barrel of his pistol down her neck. She cringed as the cold metal slid lower, as he used it to move the collar of her blouse open.

From behind her, Rosa heard Ellie's growl. Her hands were shaking, but the gun was still pointed firmly at the intruder's head. At the growl, he finally acknowledged her presence.

"Mighty big pistol there, for a little gal like you," he eyed the gun and then brought his eyes back to her face. "Bet it's startin' to get a might heavy by now. 'Fore long you'll have to drop it… or drop the baby." The words were true. Rosa saw the tension in her friend's stance, in her face. Ellie's arms were burning by then, but still she fought to keep the gun level.

Another of the men seemed to be enjoying her obvious pain. He leered at her. "We gonna get to have us some fun 'fore we take the horses to the Comanches?" His question was obviously meant for the leader, but his eyes never left

Ellie. His tongue flicked out and wet his lower lip. Ellie shuddered taking in the filth that covered him. His shirt had obvious sweat stains, frayed and yellowed from lack of washing, and dust covered every visible square inch of his being.

It was impossible to miss the disgust in Ellie's face, and the leader laughed at the question. "I think we should," he responded, turning his attention to Rosa once more. "If there's anything left of these two, we'll see what the Comanches will give for 'em." He paused, as if allowing the meaning of the words to sink in. Rosa didn't need the time. She had seen his intent displayed on his face the moment he'd knocked her down. Even now, the attraction he felt toward her was obvious, but she didn't shrink back, even as he added, "I want her first," and pushed the tip of the gun a little lower into her blouse.

Ellie growled again, and it was clear that Jeremiah had had enough. He let loose a scream that caused all three men to cringe, and proceeded to cry and wail. Ellie, having trouble balancing the gun as is, could do little to comfort him. The agony of knowing the child was frightened was written all over her face.

"Kill the damn baby first. I can't concentrate with a bawlin' kid around." Rosa saw it click. She saw the moment the battle was lost for Ellie. The desperation was so clear, making the gun even heavier in her thin arms. And, that made Rosa desperate too. She did the only thing that she could think to do. With all of the force that she could muster, she kicked upward with her foot so that it landed directly between the intruder's legs. As if in slow motion, she saw the pistol fall, heard the metal meet the floor. The shotgun quickly followed, as did the man's big frame. He crumpled to his knees in agony. The momentary distraction was all that was necessary. Before either of the other men could register what had happened, Ellie had started for the back door.

"Rosa!" She called, and tossed the pistol, before covering the baby and taking off at a full sprint. If she hadn't called out, she might have made it out of the room, but as it was, both of the men who still stood took aim and fired. Rosa's heart hurt as she saw her friend go down, the baby still clutched firmly to her breast. Anger filled her, like she had never felt before. She turned the pistol on the intruders and fired. One of the men fell, his eyes large as the realization that he had been mortally wounded by a woman took hold. Blood quickly soaked the front of him, but not before she got another shot off. The second was not as accurate. Still the second man was hit. The impact sent his return fire far to the right of Rosa, who noticed the movement of the man at her feet. He reached for the pistol.

"Dirty Mes'kin whore!" the injured man yelled from behind, firing again at Rosa, but she was quicker, emptying her pistol into him and watched him fall as well. The two fallen men did not earn a glance from their leader. He had his hands on his pistol and had eyes for only one person. Her empty gun wasn't going to do her a bit of good. Panic threatened to seize her, but the thought of Ellie and the baby gave her the inspiration to lunge for the discarded shotgun. Just as she pulled it up to his face, he had his pistol leveled at her. Suddenly the room was silent. In the midst of the standoff, Rosa wondered if she would live to see her husband again. She longed for him, for his arms to be about her one more time.

"Well now," the intruder mumbled, breaking into her thoughts. "I see now why your man would go off and leave you alone." Rosa didn't answer, but heard the cry of Ellie, and the responding cry of the baby. For a second, the gloom lifted. Her friend was still alive.

"Hold on, Ellie," She responded, filled with the desire to kill the man in front of her. The grin returned to his grimy face, which just intensified her desire to see him dead.

"Don't mind them. I'll shoot 'em quick so they don't suffer."

"Shut up," Rosa hissed in response.

"You, on the other hand," he continued. He looked her up and down, his aim not wavering in the slightest. "I was gonna take you to the Comanches with the horses, but that'd be too gentle a fate for you."

Whether because of the implications of the statement, or because of her pain, Ellie cried out again. Then she moved, and cried again, "Please, Rosa! Jeremiah is bleeding. He's bleeding bad." Her voice broke as she saw the blood puddling beneath her.

Ignoring the woman and her son, the man continued with his rant against Rosa, "No. I think I'm gonna sell you to some buffalo skinners I ran across a couple of days ago."

Rosa felt as if she were going to burst. She ignored the man before her. "Just hold on, Ellie. It'll be okay." She tried to sound comforting, confident. She wasn't, and still the man kept on.

"When they get through with you, you'd wished I'd have kept you with the horses," he taunted. "Or, maybe,

I oughta just shoot you n…" He never finished the last word. His finger shook on the trigger, but Rosa had already unloaded the shotgun directly into his chest, at point-blank range. For several moments, the only sound in the room was the whimpering of Ellie over her son. Rosa couldn't hear it anyway. She could only hear the blast reverberating in her head. She could only see the body of the third man she'd killed that day. As the haze disappeared from her mind, she was slowly able to take note of the rest of the world around her. Remembering her friend, she spared just one more second for her enemy.

"Burn in hell, Cabron," she muttered over him, then dropped the shotgun and ran to Ellie.

"Oh, Rosa…" It was all that the woman could say, but it was enough. Rosa hugged her friend, then rolled her onto her back, so she could assess the damage.

"It's going to be okay," she said, over and over again as she looked at the mother and son, both covered in blood, both faces devoid of color, "It's going to be okay."

CHAPTER FIFTEEN

STAMPEDE

THE NIGHT WAS NOT QUITE as black as usual. The moon was nearing full. Joe had watched it waxing night after night, and as it began its ascent into the sky that night, he appreciated, once again, how it continued to grow larger and larger. Hucks had pointed out the man in the moon, and ever since, Joe had been fascinated. A little piece of him wanted the man to be real, to look out for him and for his friends, as they moved the herd.

That night, Joe had not been there to bed down the horses, but he wasn't upset with Delbert for not waiting for him. The night had settled around them, as he, Johnny, and Deacon moved toward the rest of the men. Still, though, despite the late hour, the men were still eating. Around the fire, Javier, Ben, Luke, and Delbert were gathered, their supper plates still in their laps. Hucks was still working near the remnants of his cooking fire, and Joe was happy to see the man's form, as he came closer to camp.

It was Delbert who spoke first. They couldn't see the look of concern on his face, as he yelled out to them, but they could hear it in his voice. "What happened to you boys?" He called out.

Deacon waited to respond until they had come close enough to speak comfortably. "Just a little dust up with some men confused about whose cattle we were trailing." Joe looked up at him with surprise and respect.

"We took care of 'em," Johnny added.

Hucks didn't need further explanation. He turned to Deacon, "that leg need tending to?"

"Nah. Johnny looked after it already. I'll be fine." Delbert was surprised at the positive statement in relation to Johnny, but quickly wiped the evidence of the shock from his face. As the three joined the others, Johnny, Deacon and Joe fell into an easy banter, which brought a smile to Delbert's face.

As soon as Joe's plate was empty, he stood and took care of it. Then, he looked to the group. "I'm gonna go check on my remuda."

Hucks cleared his throat, turning a gruff look and tone on the boy, "You sit right back down, Joe." The ease fell from Joe's face, replaced by fear.

"Yes, sir," he mumbled, returning to his seat between Delbert and Deacon. "Did I do something wrong?"

"No. You didn't do nothin' wrong, Joe," Hucks grumbled, and shuffled something in the back of the wagon before returning to the boy, with a plate in his hand. He set it in Joe's lap.

"What's that there, Hucks?" Deacon asked.

"Peach cobbler. Made it special for you boys," Hucks responded, still looking at Joe. The boy looked down at the plate. The brightly colored peaches were piled high and topped with a golden brown cake-like crust. Even though he had just eaten, Joe felt his mouth watering at the sight. "Y'all come over and get you some," Hucks said, seeing the appreciation on Joe's face.

"Made it special? What's the occasion?" Luke asked.

Hucks finally looked away from Joe, and to Luke. "It's Joe's birthday." The surprise was immediately evident in the boy. He shot an anxious look at Hucks, then Delbert, and then Hucks again.

"I'm mighty grateful, Mr. Hucks, but..."

"Why, Joe, I didn't know it was your birthday!" Ben said, mirroring his confusion.

"Neither did I."

Again, Hucks cleared his throat "I have decided that today is Joe's birthday and we're gonna have us some fun."

"Hucks, I..." Joe said.

"Celebratin' a birthday's a might pagan, don't you think, Hucks?" Johnny spoke up. At this, the hint of embarrassment washed from Huck's. He turned a serious, if not scolding expression on Johnny.

"Well pagan or Christian, I say that ever' boy ought to know his own birthday..." He softened his tone and turned back to the boy, "and I figure that today's just as good a day as any for Joe's." The faces of all of the men turned to Joe.

"Happy birthday, Joe!" Huck added and nudged the plate a little further into Joe's lap, encouraging him to give it a try. Joe picked up the fork, still a bit uncertain.

"Happy Birthday, Joe!" The others said in unison, smiling and laughing. Joe beamed as he shoveled a huge bite of cobbler into his mouth, smiling around the sweetness. But, a moment later sadness set in.

"What's the matter, Joe?" Delbert asked, placing a hand on the small shoulder beside him.

"I'm so grateful, but it's just... It's just that I ain't never had nobody make over me like this..." he answered, his voice trailing off as his eyes searched the other faces. "I just don't know what I'm s'pose to say."

No one responded, but Delbert chuckled and patted Joe's shoulder once more. Hucks walked to his wagon and back again. Something was tucked between his arm and his side. In his opposite hand there was a package. From it he removed something and held it out to Joe.

"Now, this here is a piece of rock candy. Keep her dry if you can and knock off a piece ever' now and again. Picked it up in Ft. Worth when we passed by," he said, red coloring his bearded cheeks.

"Wow! Thanks, Mr. Hucks. I ain't never had no candy before." Hucks only nodded, then motioned for the boy to set his now empty plate aside.

"Now stand up and take off that ratty piece of trash you been wearing." The cowboy cook immediately regretted the harsh words as the boy visibly shrunk before him. Joe hesitated until Delbert gave him a gentle shove forward. Hucks pulled the bundle from under his arm and opened it to reveal a shirt.

"Now I kinda eyeballed this," he said, moving a step further from the fire as it snapped beside him. "but I think it oughta fit ya just fine."

"You made this? For me?" Joe asked, taking the proffered material and running his fingers along the clean fabric.

"It ain't much, but it'll be a sight better'n what you were wearin' anyhow," Hucks added, trying to soften the blow of his previous words. His effort was even more successful than he might have expected. Joe rushed Hucks and gives him a big hug, surprising them both.

"Oh, thank you! Thank you!" He was blushing from head to toe as he pulled away. Hucks put his hand on Joe's head, and his eyes grew misty as he looked down at him.

A ways away from the birthday celebration, watching the moon move across the sky, Emmett sat by himself. He peered over his shoulder as Delbert approached and smiled at the boys with a look of satisfaction.

"Nice evenin'," Delbert said in greeting. He moved his boot back and forth across the earth beside the other man, as if brushing away unwanted debris, then gently folded himself into a seated position. He then let his arms fall behind him, reclining into them. The moon gave the ground a luster, which made it look quite pleasant, though it had been well mowed by their herd and others that had come through. Delbert let his mind wander, thinking of the many times he had passed this same patch of prairie before. There'd been years when it had been much more lush and green, but then those were the same years that they'd lost men trying to cross the smallest creeks.

"Hope it holds," Emmett responded, calling Delbert's attention back to him. He inhaled deeply, through his nose, then turned a serious look on his friend. "Air don't quite smell right."

He didn't say anything more, but just sat in silence, alongside Delbert, recalling his own trips across that land, and the home that awaited him at the other end. As he did, he could make out bits of conversation and banter of the boys around the campfire. He could smell the sweet peaches that they consumed. He wanted to feel at peace, but something wouldn't let him settle. And, rather than being a part of the celebration, he was physically and emotionally removed. The breeze picked up around him, fluttering the short, dried clumps of grass about them. He looked back again and saw the flicker of the flames, which the men had built back up as the conversation continued. With each gust, the flames bent a bit more, and rose a bit higher between. He stood, Delbert climbing to his feet as well. Emmett looked toward the direction of the wind, and Delbert could feel Emmett's increased tension.

"Saddle up boys," he said, in a voice not much above a whisper, and then a bit louder when no one responded. The other men grumbled, and Delbert just kept looking at him. The next gust was much stronger. The camp grew silent as the coffee pot clamored to the ground before them. The pot settled finally, but the wind kept right up and the men all seemed to come back to life at once, rushing to grab their gear. Horses were quickly prepared.

"Well, this ain't worth a damn," grumbled Delbert, loud enough for Emmett to overhear. By that point, some of the cattle were snorting and in a general state of restlessness.

"All hands mount up!" Emmett cried out. "Try to hold 'em in. Things could go to hell right quick." He fought back his anxiety, the first to mount his horse. The animal pawed and spun beneath his weight.

"What about Joe?" Delbert called up to him.

A look over his shoulder at Joe made it clear that the boy was nervous but excited. Emmett's horse stilled. He was staring right at the boy when the lightning flashed behind him. Joe's silhouette was still flickering before his eyes when he looked away. "I said all hands," and he tossed another long look at the boy as he tightened the slack in the reins. The boy's face brightened, but he wasted no time hurrying after the men, jumping up on his own saddled horse.

"C'mon Rocket," he urged the beast, "we got cowboyin' to do."

Lightning struck again and the clap of thunder caused the animals' unease to increase. Joe, accustomed to late nights and early mornings thought nothing of the sleep he would be missing out on. He pulled his horse up alongside Emmett, proud to be there, one of the men. At the next sound of thunder, the horse tried to lunge, but Joe held him in check. The cattle shied in mass from the bolt of lightning that followed. The dust rose around them, billowing in clouds, which were then kicked up even more by the howling winds.

Then the rain started. Large pelting drops, blowing sideways, stung the faces and hands of the men. Joe had never seen anything like it. Emmett's horse reared and the glow of the next bolt of lightning presented a terrifying, but impressive image as Emmett moved as one with the animal.

"Stampede!" Johnny's voice rang out through the chaos.

Joe watched as the cattle started to run. One last look at the man beside him, and Joe took off on his horse at a run.

Through the wind and the rain, the men tried to make sense of the chaos as the cattle barreled forward with no destination. The herd was running as one, in sheer terror. Looking through the rain and the mess of cattle, Delbert could make out a horse and rider approaching the front of the herd.

"Who's that up there?" Delbert shouted, his voice swallowed before it had traveled to anyone but those closest to him. Luke heard him and pulled in closer to respond.

"It's Joe!" Even in the dark of night, with the lightening casting shadows over them, Delbert saw the fear in Luke's face. Mixed with it, though, was respect for the boy who had no fear.

"Go ahead on, Joe!" He screamed as loud as he could, hoping to be heard over the roar of hooves and bellowing cattle. "Turn 'em! Turn 'em!"

They couldn't see the boy anymore, but witnessed the impact that he made, as the herd began to slow. For what seemed like a lifetime, they all worked to bring the cattle around and get them to mill and quiet down. The storm blew past and the lightning strikes were seen further away, the claps of thunder losing their zeal. Delbert looked up and saw the moon.

"Man in the moon looking over us," Hucks muttered as he reined in his mount alongside Delbert. Even the Cosinero had mounted up to lend a hand in controlling the herd.

As the din died down, Emmett called them all in. Exhaustion and relief settled over him as he watched the horses approach, forming a circle about him. "Everybody here?" All heads turned from side to side, taking silent count.

"Where's Joe?" Delbert asked the question, his heart sinking as the words left his lips. In his mind, he saw again the vision of the boy, which he had witnessed for real just minutes before. The boy and his horse, Blue Rocket, the fastest horse in the remuda, were at the front of that crazed herd, trying to turn them and slow their desperate run.

"Oh, Dear Lord." Hucks circled 'round on his horse, leaving the circle, desperate to begin the hunt for the boy who had been with them, celebrating, such a short time before.

Emmett wasn't about to waste time either. Turning to Delbert, "Take who you need to keep the cattle together. Everybody else come with me," he rode without waiting for the decisions to be made.

CHAPTER SIXTEEN

BETTER MEN

J AVIER'S CHEST WAS CLENCHED SO tight he could hardly breathe. It had been several hours since the herd had been settled. They now contentedly grazed, as the sun rose over the horizon. It cast an eerie golden glow over the landscape. What had once looked so beautiful, so welcoming, suddenly caused Javier to shudder.

He guided his horse closer to the edge of a bluff which rose from a washout created by past rainstorms. For a good long while, Javier had been looking forward to the sunrise, but also dreading it.

Standing in his stirrups, he stuck two fingers between his lips and let loose an earsplitting whistle. All at once, horses and men turned toward him. Emmett was in the lead, as all moved toward him.

They reached the top of the ridge and looked down at the bottom of the ravine. Below them was a nightmare.

The boy might have looked as though he had simply laid down in the dirt to sleep off a long day on the trail, if it weren't for the horse, his head bent at an awkward angle, laid out across Joe's small body. Even from so many yards above, Javier could see the blood that had spread over his brand new shirt.

"Get him up here, boys." Emmett's voice was hollow, even in his own ears. Turning to Ben, he cleared his throat and added, "Go get me Huck's spade from the chuck wagon." He looked back down at the gruesome scene below. "I've got a hole to dig."

"We'll help you," Javier gently offered.

For a second Emmett was silent.

"No," he said finally, moving his head side-to-side, "Just me."

Ben's shoulders slumped as Emmett tossed the last spadeful of dirt atop the grave, and patted it down. Tears streamed down his cheeks. He was embarrassed to be so emotional in front of the men.

That was until he heard the sob break from Hucks' lips. The man pulled the bandana from his neck and wiped harshly at the tears, which had the nerve to overflow his eyes.

Emmett gave him a manly pat on the back, and Ben looked away.

The men gathered around the grave, some more outwardly emotional than others, but all were touched, and had very heavy hearts.

Emmett knew he had to be the one to say the words, to speak for the boy who had come into their lives and then departed so quickly. He removed his hat, as did the rest of the men.

"Lord, I know we ain't got no cause to ask why things

happen the way they do," Emmett spoke above the quiet sobs of his men. "You show us your plan on your own time. But, Joe, he…" The hitch in Emmett's voice was obvious, but no one said anything. They just stared at the mound of dirt, as their leader found his words again.

"Well, I think he made us better men." He paused, still fighting against the tears that threatened to choke him.

"So, if you'd be of a mind to take in our little stray, and let him ride with your outfit… well…" Emmett's voice quivered just as his lip did. "…we'd be much obliged."

He knelt beside the grave and touched the mound of earth that would be Joe's final resting place.

The rest of the men followed suit, each in their turn.

"God Bless Little Joe." Luke said as he touched the grave.

Emmett looked to the men and nodded.

"God Bless Little Joe," he said, barely above a whisper, before dropping his head and focusing on the lump that had formed in his chest. Calling on every last ounce of his strength, he swallowed it.

"Mount up boys. Let's get these cattle gathered and movin' 'fore we burn any more daylight."

The men didn't move, as if anchored to the spot.

"Go on now," Emmett insisted loudly, walking toward his own horse. In complete silence, the rest followed and climbed up into their own saddles. All except Hucks, who gently pushed the earth up and around a crudely made cross, carved with the inscription,

"Here lies Joe
Born around 1867
Died a Cowboy 1878"

The drive reached Abilene, Kansas at midday. Emmett swiped at the sweat on his brow with his bandana before walking into the hotel and joining the cashier at the table. The chair, with spindle legs and a small seat felt as though it would give out and drop his weight hard upon the ground at any moment.

After a brief discussion, the details were settled and Emmett nodded to the men, all lined up, one-by-one, at the door. With a brief wave of his hand, Emmett signaled for Luke, the first in line, to come forward. What might have been a moment of happy celebration on any other ride, was treated as a very somber event that day. The cashier counted out some bills and handed them to Luke.

The dainty chair was a perfect fit for the petite cashier, in his fine clothes and wire-framed spectacles. His voice, like him, was diminutive, but he enunciated well enough to be heard in the relatively quiet hotel lobby.

"Count your wages and sign the logbook," the cashier instructed, and Luke silently obeyed.

"Luke, try and actually have some of that left when you leave town, will you?" Emmett said as he battled a smile. He held out a hand, losing the battle, and it was the first smile that any of the men had seen from him since the hours before the stampede. Luke returned it with a sheepish grin of his own.

"I will, Emmett."

Johnny watched the scene unfold before him as he awaited his own pay. "Quite a trip," he said, just above a whisper, directing the comment at Deacon beside him.

"That it was," Deacon responded, a heavy sigh accentuating the words. The two stood silent for a moment, each caught up in thoughts.

"Where you headed?" Johnny finally asked.

"I believe Mr. Callaway is gonna let me winter at the Bar Nothin' again." Deacon answered before acknowledging Emmett's wave forward. He trudged forward, offering a half-smile to Emmett, then turning his eyes on the cashier. The money man glanced up, then down at the table. His placed a finger to the collar of his shirt and tugged at it slightly, as if the fabric was suddenly constricting. Then, his eyes traveled to meet Emmett's.

"He… um… he get full wages?"

Emmett narrowed his eyes and opened his mouth, prepared to answer, but it was Johnny who was heard first.

"Why wouldn't he?" He asked, shooting a glare at the nervous cashier, who once again tugged at the highest point of his shirt.

"Calm down there," the man responded, with a false harshness to his tone, and then busied himself with counting bills, never looking in Johnny's direction. "I was just making sure," he muttered just loud enough for Emmett to hear.

Emmett responded, determination in his voice. "You can be sure."

"Count it and make your mark in the logbook," the cashier said to Deacon, eyes still downcast.

"I'll sign my name," Deacon replied.

"Suit yourself," the money man responded, with more bite in his voice, the effect of which was lost given the blush coloring his cheeks.

Emmett ignored it, extending a hand to Deacon instead. "Thank you for a job well done. I wish God would bless me with a dozen of you."

"Thank you, sir," Deacon responded, pride filling his face.

Delbert smiled on, enjoying the change of attitude between Deacon and Johnny.

"I'm glad to have your help, Delbert," Javier said.

Delbert rewarded him with a bright smile. "Happy to do it, my friend. Can't think of too many ways I'd rather winter than workin' horses with you." He turned his head back to Emmett. Then, with another smile, asked, "Didn't you say that young widow of Adam's is staying at your place?"

Javier laughed and nudged Delbert's shoulder. "She is."

As the laugh died off, he reminded his friend, "Long ride back though."

"Eh, but we'll make better time driving horses. Won't be too bad."

Javier nodded.

"Javier, you're up," Emmett said.

As he walked by Johnny and Deacon, he overheard a bit of their conversation.

"Deacon, I…" Johnny started.

"I know," Deacon said, cutting off the words. "Me too." The two stood silent side-by-side, as Javier continued on past them.

"Think we'll ever ride together again?" Johnny asked Deacon, as they watched Emmett shake Javier's hand.

"Hope so."

Moments later, Delbert walked to the table for his turn.

In a repeat performance, the cashier counted and handed over a stack of bills.

"Delbert, I never regretted for a minute making you El Segundo. You'll make a fine trail boss soon. Not too many trips left in me. Maybe not any," Emmett said, as Delbert signed the logbook. Delbert set down the pen and turned a knowing glance on his boss.

Though his eyes said much more, he said only, "Thank you for the opportunity."

The two were silent as the cashier prepared for the next and last cowboy.

"Where you headed next?" Emmett asked, before Delbert could leave the table.

"Taking the remuda south with Javier. Gonna winter at his place and work horses with him," Delbert responded. Emmett smiled at the thought and extended his hand.

"Best of luck to you, Delbert."

"So long, Emmett," Delbert responded, knowing this would be the last drive with Emmett as his trail boss.

Delbert left and Ben stepped up. Ben's face showed high expectations as he looked on his uncle, but the light faded when the cashier spoke up.

"I'm sorry young man, but we've run out of cash and I'll have to pay you with a bank draft."

Ben paused for a moment, trying to comprehend what the cashier had just said.

"What does that mean?" Ben asked, looking back and forth several times between Emmett and the cashier.

"It means that you're not getting paid today, Ben," Emmett said, his tone serious even if his eyes weren't. Ben's confusion and then disappointment played out on his face.

"Unfortunately," the cashier continued, "the bank draft is drawn on the First Bank of Tarrant County. So, I'm afraid you'll have to ride back through Fort Worth on the way home."

Ben stared at the cashier, fighting the anger that welled within him. "What'd I do wrong?" He asked the question, swinging his glare on Emmett. "I worked just as hard as the other boys."

"Yes, you did, Ben. Made a much better cowboy than I expected you would."

Ben's hand came up in a gesture of confusion and anger, but Emmett just shook his head, silently telling the boy to calm down. Then, he pointed to the envelope. "There's a letter in there, Ben. It'll explain everything." He threw a knowing smile at his nephew. He just continued to grin for a moment, waiting for Ben to catch up. Then, he added, "Once you get settled in, you might send a letter of gratitude to Mr. Callaway."

"Get settled in?" Ben asked, still confused.

Emmett didn't answer, but reached in his pocket instead. He pulled out several bills and held them out to Ben. "Here's some traveling money," he said, then offered a handshake. "Good luck, son."

CHAPTER SEVENTEEN

GOING HOME

THE SUN ROSE BRIGHT THAT morning. The clouds happily dispersed leaving a crystal blue sky overhead and the earth was pleasantly pleased after a recent rain shower. Ben felt alive in a way that he hadn't the last time he had ridden through here. What he had once been uncertain of was now a memory to be called up over the many years to come. He was no longer unsure of who he was. He knew. He was a cowboy who had ridden a hard trail and come out better on the other side.

All of these thoughts were like a warm and welcome blanket over his shoulders as he dismounted and bounded up the walk. He rapped a cheerful rhythm on the heavy wooden front door, then adjusted the tie about his neck. It had taken some time to get the thing to lay correctly. It had been a while since he had had to dress in such a manner, but by the third or fourth try, he had executed a decent looking knot.

The door creaked as it was pulled open and Ben greeted Mr. Tidwell with a broad smile.

"Good morning, Mr. Tidwell."

"Do I know you, young man?" The older man asked, a hand rubbing his chin in confusion.

"I'm here to see Lucy, with your permission," Ben responded. His own hands were tucked neatly in the pockets of his pants, where he continually wiped them as nervous sweat wet his palms. It was the moment of truth as a look of recognition registered on Mr. Tidwell's face. The expression that followed was the very same that Ben had feared, but he attempted to stay strong in its presence.

"You," Tidwell growled. "You're the saddle tramp I forbade my daughter to see." His teeth ground together as the blood rushed to his face, making him look much like a tomato with whiskers. "You may have taken on a businessman's appearance, but it doesn't change who you are."

The last of the words were forced through clenched teeth, in an angry whisper as the man's daughter bounced down the stairs behind him and then slid her thin frame between her father and the door jam. Her eyes were lit and sparkling as she took in the image that Ben presented on the front step.

"Ben? Oh Ben! You came! It's really you! I knew you would. I just knew it." Her smile was contagious and Ben forgot to be fearful of the man standing behind her. He took his hand from his pocket, with one last discreet wipe of his palm, and removed his hat.

"So very nice to see you again, Miss Lucy," he said, tipping his hat to her. Lucy's radiant smile grew even larger, until she heard the angry grunt at her back.

"Oh, Father, haven't these past months softened your heart at all? Ben came back to court me, as he said he would. He kept his word," she said, spinning to address the man who had raised her.

She saw at once that the man had not softened at all. Instead, it was as if every part of him had grown harder in the short time that Ben had stood on the stoop. He addressed his daughter in a voice not much warmer than that he had turned on the young man.

"And, I will keep mine." His feet were heavy as he walked away at a brisk pace.

Ben was momentarily taken aback, believing that he might have an opportunity to speak privately with the young woman who had so quickly worked her way into his heart. His sentiments quickly altered, however, as he stood, staring down both barrels of Tidwell's shotgun.

Lucy at once tried to push herself between the two men, but Ben gently moved her aside, standing between the girl and her father.

"I told you not to come back," the older man spat at him, "and I told you that you were not to ever see my daughter again."

Ben bravely turned his eyes from the gun, to peer at Lucy. He offered her a reassuring smile, then, looking back at the man wielding the weapon spoke, "Lucy, forgive me for what I'm about to do." He quickly pulled his pistol from the holster slung low on his hip and pointed it directly at Tidwell's heart, which was, Ben figured, the part of the man that he must appeal to. "Mr. Tidwell, please, put down the shotgun before we are left to regret what happens."

By this point, sweat had started to form at the other man's forehead. "You... you, you, you scamp!" He huffed.

"I'm here to court your daughter. I ask you again, as I

did before, for your permission to do so," Ben began in a gentler voice, one with unmistakable respect for his elder. Though he did not allow anyone to mistake his serious stance. "But, with or without your permission, if she is still willing, we will court." He waited a second and seeing no evidence of a change of heart, he urged again. This time he moved the pistol just slightly, up and down, to emphasize his words. "Put down the shotgun, Mr. Tidwell."

It was an endless few moments, as the men faced off in a battle of wills. It was, though, Mr. Tidwell, who finally lowered his weapon. Ben waited until the gun had been handed to Lucy, who held it tightly, before he lowered his own gun and returned it to its holster. Still, there was a very heavy silence, as the sun shone down on the scene.

Ben cleared his throat, and without taking his eyes off of the father, addressed the daughter, "Lucy, I received your letter and was overjoyed by it." Despite the nervousness, a slight smile tugged at the corner of his lips as he recalled the joy that had surged through him when first reading her words. He had read it several dozen times since, until he had it memorized word-for-word. The happiness did not pass to Tidwell who turned a scowl on his daughter.

"What letter?"

Ignoring the question, Ben continued on, "Do you still feel as you said?" He asked, even more greatly concerned about what her answer might be than he had been when staring at the wrong end of the shotgun.

"I do, Ben," she said, and so much glee filled Ben's chest that it threatened to choke him, making it nearly impossible to comprehend the rest of her words, "I said I would bear the scandal of courting without my father's permission, and I will do so..." looking up at her father, she added, "with a joyful heart."

Ben's chuckle might have been considered a giggle by some, and for that reason, he was happy that the other cowboys weren't present to hear it. "I'm staying in Fort Worth. I'm going to make it my home, just as it is yours."

Lucy started forward, then, remembering the weapon that she held, she slipped into the house, returning a moment later without it. "It's wonderful, Ben!" She stepped in front of her father, close enough to hug him, but had enough restraint not to do so. "But how? What will you do?"

"I liked the trail. The cattle. The horses. Especially the company of the men on the drive, but I'm staying put.

I am apprenticed to Mr. John Ferguson, Senior Officer of the First Bank of Tarrant County." He stood taller then, the pride evident in his face, "Mr. Callaway, who owns the Bar Nothin' Ranch, recommended me. Mr. Ferguson agreed to my situation, sight unseen." From the corner of his eye, Ben saw the anger fall away from Tidwell's face, to be replaced by confusion.

"Oh Ben!" Lucy exclaimed, and this time her hand did reach out and touch him. It wasn't a full hug, but it was enough to bring another layer of warmth to Ben's skin.

"In a year or two, I will be a full clerk," he said, feeling the need to continue as he stared into the eyes of the beautiful woman before him, "It's a great opportunity for such a young man as myself."

Finally he tore his eyes from Lucy's.

"Mr. Tidwell, Ft. Worth is growing and thriving, in part because of successful businessmen like you. I am happy to have a part in helping foster that growth."

Receiving no response, but seeing the clear signs of respect written on the other man's face, Ben took a chance, "Miss Lucy? Would you be willing to take a walk with me?" Giving Tidwell a sidelong glance, he added, "Not far. Just a short walk." She grasped his arm as soon as he offered it and he paid her with the biggest smile he had ever bestowed on another person.

Lucy looked back at her father, briefly. His look in response was one of resignation, but it was obvious that it was enough because there was a distinct and graceful bounce to Lucy's stride as she walked away on the arm of the cowboy turned banker.

Delbert was correct in his estimation that the return trip would be much faster. The remuda seemed to know what was coming at the end of the trip and moved with ease toward the reward of grazing pastures and a comfortable barn. So, despite a large number of four-legged companions, the two men made their trip in good time and were coming upon Javier's ranch wearing smiles.

The sun was at their faces as they approached, so the house and barn were silhouetted, but Javier didn't miss the movement of his wife exiting the front door and walking toward him. She paused her steps on the front porch. He could make out her figure bending slightly and then moving toward the front gate. For the first time since he had left her in their bed, Javier's heart felt light. He urged his horse, pressing his knees together just slightly. The animal started forward at a faster walk, but it was still too slow for Javier. Delbert noticed.

"Javier," he said, looking at his companion, then lifted his head toward the house. "Go ahead. I can bring 'em in from here. They'll be eager to join the other horses up at the barn anyway." His smile broadened as he urged his friend again, his hand making a shooing motion.

Javier could hear her voice on the wind as he drew nearer, but couldn't make out her words. He didn't need to. The sight of her was enough. Her once thin frame was bulging at the center. A round protruding stomach told him that his dreams were coming true. He heard a smaller voice, but paid it no attention as he stared at his wife's center.

"Wait there, dulce nina," Rosa said to the toddler, her face turned momentarily away from Javier. And, then, turning to him as he finally reached his home she yelled, "Javi! My Javi!"

The joy in her expression was complete and heartfelt. Tears began to stream down her face as she bounced in her shoes. The horse hadn't even come to a full stop when Javier threw his legs over and leapt to the ground. In two strides, he was at her side, pulling her swelling frame into his own.

After a moment of holding her tight and close, he pulled away, "Rosa?" He asks the question with eyes lowered to her abdomen.

"We are Blessed, Javi! Blessed!" She responded through a large smile, and tears that continued to wet her face as the relief washed over her.

"Gracias a Dios! What a welcome!"

She let him say no more, pulling him close once more. "Oh how I missed you!"

The laughter began as a rumble in his chest and burst

through his lips, which he then lowered to her head, kissing her hairline and then each cheek. "And I you."

The sounds of the remuda joining Javier's other horses, and Delbert's whistle as he worked them through the gate to the large corral, pulled Javier from his moment of bliss. It didn't, however, take away the happy warmth that had filled him. He looked to the corral and saw that the horses were welcoming the ranch as eagerly as he had. Then, he glanced to the porch, and found the source of the small voice he had heard before.

The boy was just a toddler, but this was such a transformation from when he had left that it took a moment for it sink in. "Jeremiah?" The boy jabbered away in response, with words that made no sense to anyone but him. "Where's Ellie?" Javier asked his wife, smiling at the boy.

For the first time since she had come into his view, he saw the joy fade from Rosa. Her shoulders slumped forward and another tear pushed forth from her eye. He suspected that it was not a result of the same emotion as the others had been.

"What happened, Rosa?" He asked the question lowering himself with bent knees and lifting her chin simultaneously, so their eyes met again. She attempted another smile, but this one felt forced and he saw through it. His eyes asked the question again.

"Comancheros," she muttered at last. The emotional turmoil filling her as she recalled the devastation that had followed the invasion. "Some Comancheros came to take the horses... and to take us." Javier's knees straightened and Rosa could feel his anger, but she stopped him with a hand.

"They are dead, Javier. We fought them. But, they killed Ellie. She died holding her baby boy," she said, collapsing into his chest. "I couldn't save her."

Javier said nothing for several moments. The two walked up onto the front porch together, hand-in-hand. All the while, Javier held his wife, grieving with her. "We haven't seen Comancheros around here for years," he said, almost too quietly for her to here, as if trying to justify his leaving.

Rosa pulled away, wiped her tears and looked at him with an expression of strength. "I know. We haven't, Javi. It's not your fault."

"And, it's not yours," he added.

"You will keep your word?" she asked, after a pause. "No more trips north?"

"No, Rosa," he responded, shaking his head for emphasis, "no more trips north. I will keep my word." And, he wrapped her in his warmth once more, before adding, "We will soon have two children to look after. You would be outnumbered without me." The feeling of her chuckle against him was the greatest homecoming gift that he could have asked for.

She spun around so that she rested at his side, with his arm resting upon her shoulders, as they started for the house. "Was that Delbert bringing in the horses?"

"Si. He made the trip back with me. He'll stay for the winter." He looked at her with a question in his eyes. She smiled back and gave an affirmative nod.

"Good. It is good."

As they stood together, Javier brought his other arm

around and placed a hand on her rounded belly. Rosa laughed and then smiled at him.

"Ellie for a girl, but I have a name I'd like to give him… if it's a son."

"What is it, Javi?" She asked.

He turned to look directly in her eyes once more, "Jose… Joe."

EPILOGUE

Little Joe the Wrangler (The Original Poem)

Little Joe, the wrangler, will never wrangle more;
His days with the "Remuda" — they are done.
'Twas a year ago last April he joined the outfit here,
A little "Texas Stray" and all alone.

'Twas long late in the evening he rode up to the herd
On a little old brown pony he called Chaw;
With his brogan shoes and overalls a harder looking kid
You never in your life had seen before.

His saddle 'twas a southern kack built many years ago,
An O.K. spur on one foot idly hung,
While his "hot roll" in a cotton sack was loosely tied behind
And a canteen from the saddle horn he'd slung.

He said he'd had to leave his home, his daddy'd married twice
And his new ma beat him every day or two;

*So he saddled up old Chaw one night and "Lit a shuck"
this way*
   Thought he'd try and paddle now his own canoe.

   *Said he'd try and do the best he could if we'd only give
him work*
   Though he didn't know "straight" up about a cow,
   So the boss he cut him out a mount and kinder put him on
   For he sorter liked the little stray somehow.

   *Taught him how to herd the horses and to learn to know
them all*
   To round 'em up by daylight; if he could
   To follow the chuck-wagon and to always hitch the team
   And help the "cosinero" rustle wood.

   We'd driven to red river and the weather had been fine;
   We were camped down on the south side in a bend
   *When a norther commenced to blowing and we doubled
up our guards*
   For it took all hands to hold the cattle then.

   Little Joe the wrangler was called out with the rest
   And scarcely had the kid got to the herd
   *When the cattle they stampeded; like a hail storm, long
they flew*
   And all of us were riding for the lead.

   *"Tween the streaks of lightning we could see a horse far
out ahead*
   'Twas little Joe the wrangler in the lead;

He was riding old "Blue Rocket" with his slicker 'bove his head
    Trying to check the leaders in their speed.

At last we got them milling and kinder quieted down
And the extra guard back to the camp did go
But one of them was missin' and we all knew at a glance
'Twas our little Texas stray, poor wrangler Joe.

Next morning just at sunup we found where Rocket fell
Down in a washout twenty feet below
Beneath his horse mashed to a pulp, his spur had rung the knell
For our little Texas stray — poor wrangler Joe.

Jack Thorpe
1908